500
things to know about
THE ANCIENT
WORLD

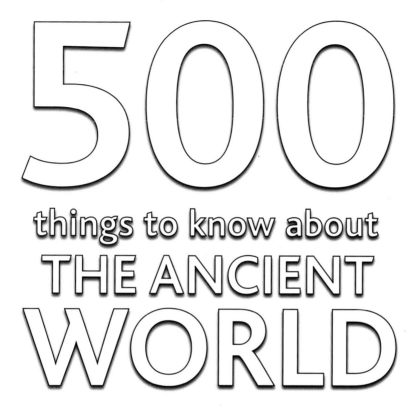

500

things to know about
THE ANCIENT
WORLD

Carolyn Howitt

BARRON'S

To Lewis and Ines

First edition for the United States, its territories and dependencies, and Canada published in 2007 by Barron's Educational Series, Inc.

© Copyright 2007 by The Trustees of the British Museum
Published by British Museum Press
A division of The British Museum Company, Ltd.
38 Russell Square, London WC1B 3QQ, United Kingdom

Carolyn Howitt has asserted her right to be identified as the author of this work in accordance with British law.

All photographs and artwork © copyright The Trustees of the British Museum unless otherwise noted below.

The Trustees of the British Museum and Barron's would like to acknowledge the following individuals whose images appear in this book: Lesley and Roy Adkins, p. 136 (bottom); John Green, p. 67; Patricia Hansom, pp. 27, 34 (top), 51 (bottom), 55 (bottom), 115 (bottom), and 145 (top); Graham Harrison, p. 126; Karen Hughes, p. 131; Ann Searight, pp. 82 (top) and 125 (bottom); and Chris West (Black Hat Agency), p. 113 (bottom).

All inquiries should be addressed to:
Barron's Educational Series, Inc.
250 Wireless Boulevard
Hauppauge, NY 11788
www.barronseduc.com

Library of Congress Control Number: 2007921750

ISBN-13: 978-0-7641-3863-8
ISBN-10: 0-7641-3863-4

Printed and bound in China
9 8 7 6 5 4 3 2 1

Start here to discover 500 of the most amazing facts about the people, places, and things of the past – all collected from the experts at the British Museum. Choose a chapter that interests you, or just open the book and dip in. Have fun!

Contents

Animals

1 An ancient Egyptian farmer called one of his cows *Mehet-weret*, "Great-Flood." It was crucial for Egyptian farmers that the River Nile should flood well each year and make the soil fertile so that their crops would grow.

2 One Egyptian man from Thebes called his dog *En-mereni* (which means "I don't like anybody!").

TEN FACTS
about cats in ancient Egypt

3 The word for cat in Egyptian was *miu*.

4 Pet cats are often shown in tomb paintings sitting under their owner's chairs.

5 Cats were sacred to the goddess Bastet, who is often shown as a woman with a cat's head.

6 Sacred cats were mummified by the thousands and buried in special cemeteries.

7 Some mummies contain incomplete cat skeletons, so people who paid for cat mummies to offer to the goddess were ripped off.

8 One ancient writer said that when a cat died, its owners shaved their eyebrows off in mourning.

9 The sun-god was sometimes believed to appear in the form of a cat. Egyptian Books of the Dead sometimes showed a cat killing the serpent Apophis, the sun-god's enemy.

10 Seeing a large cat in a dream was lucky, and meant there would be a good harvest.

11 A famous Wisdom Text giving advice on how to live a good life says, "Do not laugh at a cat."

12 Egyptians out hunting birds trained their cats to fetch back the birds they had shot down with arrows.

Mummy of a cat from Abydos, Egypt, 1st century A.D.

13

Baboons were sometimes trained by the Egyptians to help them pick fruit at harvest time.

Copy of a painting from the tomb of Knumhotep at Beni Hasan.

14

The scarab beetle lays its eggs in a ball of dung, then rolls the ball along wherever it goes. When the young beetles hatch, it looks as if they are miraculously coming out of the dung. Egyptians thought the scarab beetle symbolized rebirth.

Scarab amulet from Egypt, 1550–1069 B.C.

15

There were no rabbits in ancient Egypt. This hieroglyphic sign actually shows a hare.

16

Rabbits are not native to Britain. They have long been thought to have been introduced by the Normans in 1066. However, archaeologists have found the remains of a meal including rabbit bones on a Roman site in eastern England. Did the Romans bring rabbit stew with them when they invaded in 43 A.D.?

17

Early inhabitants of Britain, such as Celts and Anglo-Saxons, did not have pets in the same way that we do today. All animals had a use, so dogs were kept for hunting and cats for catching mice.

18

There were wolves in Anglo–Saxon England. They were feared because they were dangerous animals, but also admired as being brave and strong.

19

Many ancient Minoan pictures show the dangerous sport of bull-leaping, in which young men and women somersaulted over the horns of a charging bull.

Bronze bull and acrobat from Minoan Crete, about 1700–1450 B.C.

20

In ancient China, fishermen used cormorants to help them catch fish. Lamps shining from their boats attracted fish to the surface of the water, where the birds swooped down and picked them up. Neck collars stopped them from eating the fish, which the fishermen then took away from them. This kind of fishing is still practiced in parts of China today.

21

There were no horses in North America until the Spanish brought them in the 16th century. The Native Americans weren't allowed to buy any, but they managed to get hold of strays, or steal some. The arrival of the horse completely changed their way of life. Now they could travel long distances, and hunting was much easier.

22

The Native American peoples who lived on the plains of North America depended on buffalo for their living. They used every part of the animal, eating the meat, using the skins for tipi covers and clothes, and the bones for tools. There were around fifty million buffalo when the Europeans first arrived, but by the end of the 1880s, white settlers had killed nearly all of them: there were less than 1,000 buffalo left.

Blackfoot buffalo robe from North America, before 1868 A.D.

Strange creatures of legend

SEVEN FACTS
about dragons

23 Dragons are international. Stories about them have been told in many cultures for thousands of years.

24 One of the earliest references to a dragon is the *mushhushshu*, or "furious snake," who is said to have guarded the ancient city of Babylon.

25 Often dragons appear frightening or evil, but Chinese dragons are viewed as a symbol of good luck.

26 Chinese dragons are usually shown with three or four claws. Only the emperor and his family could wear clothes or use objects decorated with five-clawed dragons.

A five-clawed dragon on a Chinese enamel jar, Ming Period 1426–35 A.D.

Dragon figurehead from a ship, 4th–6th century A.D.

27 Some Germanic peoples used fierce dragon carvings as the figureheads on their ships. Sea journeys were dangerous and the dragons were meant to scare away evil forces.

28 The night before St. Margaret died (so the story goes), the Devil appeared to her in the form of a dragon. It swallowed her, but the cross she was wearing stuck in its throat and it was forced to cough her out.

29 St. George was a Roman soldier in Palestine around 300 A.D. Sadly, he probably never killed a dragon.

Icon of St. George and the dragon, from Russia, late 14th century A.D.

FIVE
mixed-up creatures

Many cultures have stories about creatures made from the body parts of different animals.

30 The griffin (ancient Greece and Persia) had the head and wings of an eagle and the body, feet, and claws of a lion. Greek griffins had spikes on their heads.

31 The Devourer (ancient Egypt) was part crocodile, part lion, and part hippo. The Devourer ate anyone who didn't make it past the judges into the afterlife.

Lion–griffin ornament from the Oxus treasure, Achaemenid Persian from Tadjikistan, 5th–4th century B.C.

The Devourer. From the papyrus of Ani, around 1275 B.C.

32 Chimaera: the ancient Etruscans and Greeks told stories about these creatures, which could be part lion, part goat, part snake, and also had wings.

33 Hippocamp: a Greek sea creature, half horse, half fish, with a serpent's tail.

34 Sphinx: in ancient Egypt, the sphinx had the body of a lion and the head of another creature, often (but not always) human.

Hawk-headed sphinx from Egypt, about 1250 B.C.

35

Pegasus was the famous winged horse of ancient Greek legend. He sprang from the blood of the snake-haired monster Medusa when she was slain by Perseus.

36

Chinese mythical beasts called *qilins* were thought to announce the birth of a genius child, so pictures of them were often put near cradles for good luck.

Chinese jade phoenix, 10th–11th century A.D.

38

In legend, the beautiful phoenix bird lays a single egg on its funeral pyre before it dies. It is then born again from the egg in the flames. In Chinese legend, the phoenix is simply immortal.

37

When the Mayans of ancient Mexico killed an animal while hunting they would apologize to the god of hunting, and explain exactly why they had done it. The Mayans believed that if they killed more animals than they needed, the god of hunting would be angry and not let them catch any animals the next time.

Death

After you died in ancient

ROME

39 Romans thought it was lucky to breathe in the last gasp of a dying person. The eldest Roman male family member would be summoned to the bedside to try to inhale it.

40 Dead people were laid out in their houses for a week. They could get very smelly during this time!

41 A dead body was taken to a cemetery. Family members made up a procession alongside wearing masks showing the faces of dead ancestors.

Tomb portraits of a married couple who lived in Rome during the reign of the emperor Augustus.

42

The Roman emperor Septimius Severus (reigned 193–211 A.D.) died in York, so a wax effigy was made of his body so that it could go through the funeral rites back in Rome. This waxwork was treated by doctors as if it were dying, then it took part in several ceremonies. Finally it was placed on a huge funeral pyre made up of several wooden levels, like a huge wedding cake. As the flames took hold, an eagle was released from the top of the pyre, "taking the soul of the emperor from earth to heaven."

Marble statue of the emperor Septimius Severus in military uniform.

43 Romans built funeral pyres out of logs, with the body placed high up on top. The corpse's eyes were left open so the dead person could see the heavens. At one funeral, according to the writer Pliny, the flames were so fierce that the body was thrown off the pyre. The family could not get it to stay on the pyre because the heat was too great.

44 Rich Romans would sometimes pay for professional mourners to join their funeral processions. Their perfect wailing and moaning would add just the right touch to the occasion.

Death in ancient Egypt

EGYPTIAN MUMMIES

45 The Egyptians believed that after death you needed your actual body to use in the afterlife. They conceived of a way to preserve bodies called mummification. Only rich, important people could afford to be mummified. The word "mummy" comes from Arabs who settled in Egypt in the seventh century A.D. They looked inside some of the tombs and noticed that the bodies were covered in black sticky stuff, which they thought was bitumen; the Arabic word for bitumen is *mummia*.

The mummy and coffin of Ankhef, an official of the Middle Kingdom period.

Mummy of Cleopatra, a young girl from Thebes, Egypt, 2nd century A.D. (This is not the famous queen Cleopatra!)

46 HOW TO MAKE A MUMMY

WARNING
THIS IS DEFINITELY NOT SOMETHING TO TRY AT HOME.

1 Take the brain out in pieces through the nose and throw it away; the ancient Egyptians didn't think the brain performed any inportant functions.

Probe used to remove the brain.

2 Cut a deep slash across the lower left stomach. Through this, pull out the liver, lungs, stomach, and intestines.

3 Dry these organs out, cover them with natron salt and resin (gum from coniferous trees), wrap them in linen, then put them back into the corpse. In the early days of mummy-making, one would place the organs into special canopic jars, which were buried with the mummy.

4 Whatever you do, don't touch the heart. It is the soul of the person.

5 The eyes will shrivel up. Replace them with stone or glass eyes so the person can see in the afterlife.

6 Cover the body with natron salt and pack more inside. Leave it for about forty days until all moisture is gone.

7 Fill up the empty spaces inside the body with rolls of cloth, spices, or sawdust, and coat the body with melted resin.

8 Wrap the body in layer after layer of linen strips and sheets. Place in wooden coffin.

Wooden coffin of Hornedjitef, a priest from Thebes, with a gilded face. 3rd century B.C.

47 The Egyptians sometimes mummified their pets and other animals, as well as their relatives. From about 747 B.C., many different animals were mummified, including crocodiles, eels, baboons, falcons, jackals, and bulls. It was thought that these creatures were representations of the gods on earth.

Mummy of a jackal or dog from Thebes, Egypt, after 30 B.C.

Death customs around the world

48 A Viking warrior's body could be placed on his ship when he died and the whole thing set alight with flaming arrows before being cast off to drift on the waves.

49 "Earth laid upon a corpse" is an ancient Scottish funeral custom. The body was buried with a plate of earth and salt on its chest. Earth showed that the body would decay, but salt represented the soul, which would continue on.

50 Jade has always been very valuable in China. People believed that it stopped dead bodies from rotting. At one time jade was used to plug up all the holes in a corpse, and a jade cicada (similar to a grasshopper) was placed on the tongue.

Jade cicada from China, Han dynasty, 206 B.C.–220 A.D.

Lindow Man as he looks today. He died mid-1st century A.D.

51 Lindow Man's body (a naturally-made mummy found in modern times) was found in Lindow Moss, a peat bog in Cheshire, northern England. The young man had been gruesomely killed in a special ceremony—first he was struck hard on the head and in the back, and a thick cord around his neck strangled him and broke his neck. By this time he was probably dead, but then his throat was cut. Finally he was placed face down in the peat.

52 There is some evidence that Viking warriors sacrificed (probably willing) slave girls to become their wives in the afterlife.

Human sacrifice

53

The ancient Greeks did not practice human sacrifice, although it sometimes happens in Greek myths. In the story of the Trojan War, the Greek general Agamemnon was forced to sacrifice his daughter Iphigenia to the goddess Artemis. In another version of the story, Iphigenia gets saved at the last minute.

54

Slaves were buried alive to serve their masters and mistresses in the afterlife in the ancient Chinese Shang and Zhou dynasties.

55

Early Roman sacrificial victims have been found buried in the foundations of buildings. Perhaps it was thought they gave the buildings strength?

56

Self-sacrifice (cutting or piercing your own body so that it bled) was common among the Aztecs, and was thought to be another way to offer blood to the gods and keep them happy.

57

To keep the sun moving across the sky, the Aztecs believed it needed to be nourished with the blood of sacrificial victims. Prisoners taken in battle would be killed on special occasions, sometimes in the thousands. They would be thrown over a stone altar, their hearts pierced with a special knife, then their bodies were thrown down the steep temple steps. Skulls would be displayed outside the temple on racks.

Aztec sacrificial knife. The handle is made of turquoise mosaic. 15th–16th century A.D.

Animal sacrifice

58

The Ashvamedha (horse sacrifice) was one of the most important royal rituals of the Vedic (ancient Hindu) religion. It could only be carried out by a king. The horse was sprinkled with water, then set free to roam for a year. It was followed by a hundred young men who watched closely where it went. All the lands it went through then belonged to the king. On its return, the horse was bathed, anointed, and decorated.

Gold coin showing the tethered horse used in the Ashvamedha ritual of King Kumaragupta I, around 415–50 A.D.

The horse was then tied to a stake with 17 other animals attached to it and slaughtered. The queen would spend the night with the dead animal before it was roasted the next day.

59

Sometimes Aztecs killed a dog at funerals so that the dog's soul could lead the soul of the dead person safely through the underworld.

60

In ancient Rome, animals were frequently sacrificed to the gods because it was believed that this was the best way of keeping them happy. The demand for sacrificial animals (especially pigs and cattle) was so great that a special market selling them sprang up in Rome.

61

Making a sacrifice to the gods was a very important part of ancient Greek religion. A bull, sheep, goat, or other animal was led to the altar in a procession, then sacrificed. The bones and fat were offered to the gods, and the humans ate the good meat themselves.

A young cow being led to the altar, from the South Frieze of the Parthenon. Around 438–432 B.C.

Medea offering a ram to the gods. A red-figure vase.

17

Afterlife beliefs

62

The Greeks believed that Charon ferried the souls of the dead across the river Styx to Hades, the underworld. But Charon had to be paid, or he would not row the soul over the river! So the Greeks put a coin in a dead person's mouth as payment. In Greek mythology, the far side of the river was guarded by the three-headed dog Cerberus.

Charon the ferryman, on a white-ground vase.

63

The Greek underworld took its name from the god Hades, who ruled it.

64

Ancient Romans also believed in Hades as the underworld, but they called the god who ruled it Pluto. Charon still rowed souls across the river, they believed, to be judged.

65

Two thousand years before the ancient Greeks, the ancient Sumerians believed that the dead were ferried across a river in a boat to the next world. This world was either beneath the earth or above it.

66

The Maya believed that there was an underworld with nine levels. One's soul had to undertake a dangerous journey through these levels after one died. The worst one was called *Metnal* and was ruled over by Ah Puch, the god of death. He was depicted as a skeleton hung with bells.

67

The Aztecs believed in a well-ordered life after death in a place called *Mictlan*, which was on nine different levels. The soul of a dead person would go to a different level according to how he or she had died. Death was just a gateway and not to be feared at all. There were also special paradises especially for children, for men who had died in battle, and for women who had died in childbirth.

Statue of the Aztec god of the dead, MIctlantecuhtli.

68

The ancient Egyptians believed that after death, one's soul had to go on a journey through the underworld, a place full of terrifying monsters and many dangers. A copy of the *Book of the Dead* could help one through this by giving one the right spells to say. If one survived the journey, one's heart was weighed against a feather, which stood for "right" or "truth." If it did not balance, then one's soul was eaten by the fierce Devourer, part crocodile, part lion, and part hippopotamus.

Animal-headed demons guarding the gates to the Egyptian underworld.

Sinners run from Hell toward
Kshitigarbha, who has the
power to save them. China,
late 9th–early 10th century A.D.

A large Ming porcelain figure of
an assistant to the judge of Hell,
made around 1522–1620 A.D.

69

A paper roll painting in the
British Museum shows the
10 Buddhist "Kings of Hell."
The Buddhists believed that
the kings judged people's
souls to see what they
should be reborn as in their
next lives. There are six *gati*
(ways of rebirth), in the
following order:

1. Ways of divine beings
2. Titanic demons
3. Men
4. Animals
5. Hungry ghosts
6. Hell

70

When brave warriors died, Vikings
believed that their souls went to a big
hall called Valhalla, or "Hall of the
Slain." Valhalla had 540 doors, walls
made of spears, and a roof made of
shields. Every day the dead warriors
fought mock battles, and every night
they feasted.

71

The name Hell comes from Hel in
Norse mythology. Hel was the goddess
of the underworld, which also took
her name. It was a miserable place,
surrounded by a freezing river full of
knives. The souls of the dead crossed
over a bridge guarded by a giantess. In
Hel they waded through rivers of
blood, serpents' poison dripped on
them from the roof, and they could
only drink goat's urine.

Tombs and graves

72

When the Sumerian Queen Pu-abi died, her corpse was richly dressed and laid on a wooden stand, with a gold cup by her hand. Teams of oxen harnessed to vehicles were then buried with her, as well as 90 attendants in their best clothes, laid out in rows. The Great Death Pit nearby also held six servants, four harpists, and sixty-four other beautifully dressed women. They may have all taken poison, or were buried when they were already dead or unconscious. Pu-abi was buried about 2600 B.C. in one of the royal graves found at Ur, Mesopotamia (modern Iraq).

Queen Pu-abi's golden headdress, made about 2600 B.C.

73

The Hopewell people of North America lived around 100 B.C. in the area that is now Ohio. They were successful farmers who built large earthworks. Some of these may have been used to hold ceremonies; others are burial mounds where important people were laid to rest, surrounded by tools and beautiful jewelry.

74

Like the Egyptians, the Chinese thought that the afterlife was like real life, and that persons could take objects with them if models of the things were left in their tomb. These could sometimes be life-sized.

Bullock pulling a cart, 45 cm high tomb model from China, 6th century A.D.

SEVEN FACTS
about Egyptian tombs

Box of *shabtis* from the tomb of a woman called Henutmehyt, around 1250 B.C.

75 Most New Kingdom Egyptian rulers were buried in a place called the Valley of the Kings in elaborate tombs cut into the rock and filled with treasures.

76 Egyptian tombs were full of precious objects, models, and pictures. Ancient Egyptians believed that people could use the things buried with them in the afterlife. For example, model boats were buried to help the person's soul on its journey through the next world.

77 Offerings of food and drink were given to the dead. The Egyptians thought that the spirit of the person could eat the food if it was in his or her tomb.

78 Egyptians buried model servants called *shabtis* with the dead to serve them in the afterlife.

79 Coffins and tombs were inscribed with hieroglyphic spells to help the dead person on his or her journey to paradise.

80 Tomb robbers, from ancient Egyptian times to the present day, have stolen the tomb goods from many Egyptian tombs.

81 The only Egyptian king's tomb to escape the tomb robbers was that of Tutankhamun.

Food offerings found in an Egyptian tomb.

82

Roman cemeteries had to be outside towns by law, mainly because of the risk of disease. Cemeteries were often laid out alongside main roads. On certain days of the year, offerings of food and drink were given to the dead—these could be put down tubes into the graves.

83

In Roman times, Christians and Jews, and even some pagan Romans, sometimes buried their dead in underground caves called "catacombs." The Christian catacombs in Rome are the most famous today. As well as providing cheap and plentiful graveyard space, the catacombs were used for meetings and ceremonies.

84

A fascinating woman was buried at Wetwang in Yorkshire, England, in the Iron Age. The woman was 5 ft 9 in (1.75 m) tall and had a badly scarred face. She also had a dislocated shoulder, meaning that in real life she couldn't have actually driven the chariot she was buried in. In Iron Age Britain, important people sometimes seem to have been buried with chariots.

85

Powerful rulers were sometimes buried inside their ships in Anglo–Saxon England. The most famous of these burials is at Sutton Hoo in Suffolk. An oaken ship, 97 feet (30 m) long, was deeply buried beneath a large grassy mound. Inside the ship, a dead man was laid, surrounded by his weapons and other precious objects. The ship has rotted away, but the outline of her planks and iron rivets was preserved in the sandy soil.

The outline of the Sutton Hoo ship preserved in the sand, as it was found in 1939.

Helmet from the ship burial at Sutton Hoo in England, early 7th century A.D.

Family life

86

The ancient Egyptian words for "son" and "daughter" were written with bird hieroglyphs and may really have meant "chick."

"Son"   "Daughter"

87

The Egyptians valued children highly, and families often had between five and ten children, but the death rate among children was very high.

88

The Aztecs said that a baby was like a jewel or a precious flower. When an Aztec baby was born, there were celebrations lasting several days. They thought that having children was one of the most important things someone could do.

89

Aztec children had several names. One name was always the birth date, such as 1 Flower. People thought the day decided the child's future. A child born on 2 Rabbit might be a drunkard!

90

Aztecs were very loving but very strict parents. They punished children when they misbehaved. One book shows parents holding children over a fire of chilis, and pricking them with cactus spines. We don't know if they really did anything so cruel!

An Aztec parent and child over a fire of chilis.

24

91 ELEVEN EGYPTIAN NAMES
and what they mean

Ramesses:	The sun god has given birth to him
Aapehty:	Great of strength
Meresankh:	May she love life
Wereshunefer:	The one who spends the day happy
Dersenedj:	The one who wards away fear
Desheri:	Red
Anemher:	Gorgeous
Webennesiah:	The moon shines for her
Bia:	Miracle
Meretites:	She who loves her father
Seshen:	Lotus flower (an ancient Egyptian version of the modern name Susan)

92 Vikings did not have surnames like we do. Instead they were named after their fathers, and part of their name said whether they were his son or daughter. A family tree might look like this:

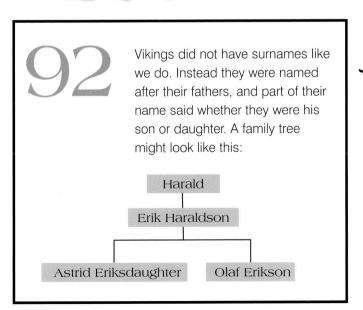

93

Roman fathers literally owned the rest of the family and made all the decisions.

25

94

In ancient Athens, a woman was expected to look after the home and have children. Women could not inherit property. So if a woman had no brothers, when her father died she might have to marry her father's brother to keep the estate in the family.

A small child crawling toward its mother, on a Greek pot.

Mother and child from a Ming Period woodblock print, 17th century A.D.

95

Chinese ages were counted from one rather than zero, so Chinese babies were considered to be one year old the day they were born. They would then add a year to their age at the next Chinese New Year, instead of having a birthday (this meant that a child born on New Year's Eve could be two years old the next day!).

96

FIVE ANGLO–SAXON NAMES
and what they mean

Gertrude: spear strength

Alfred: elf counsel

Hilda: battle maid

Edward: guardian of wealth

Unready: badly advised, "without counsel"
(as in King Ethelred the Unready)

An Anglo–Saxon home.

Wedding bells

97

Roman marriages were mostly arranged by families. Women had very little say in the decision about who they married. They were often given as brides as young as 12 to much older men.

98

Girls of 13 or 14 were married to men of about 30 in ancient Greece, although women in Sparta had more equality and probably married later.

Carving of a Roman wedding ceremony.

A Greek wedding procession, painted on a vase.

99 During the Ptolemaic period in Egypt (332–30 B.C.), kings married their sisters and declared that they were gods.

100 When a young Mayan man got married, he would work for his wife's family for about six years. After this, the couple went to live with or near the husband's family.

101 In ancient China, a man could have only one main wife. She shared his honors, but he was also free to take lesser wives, called concubines, to ensure that he had more children. He could have many concubines. These second-class wives could be very badly treated by their husbands and the chief wives.

A lady waiting in vain for her husband to arrive. Qing Dynasty hanging scroll, 19th century A.D.

102 In ancient China, marriages were arranged by professional matchmakers, sometimes before the bride and groom were even born! A bride had to become a member of her husband's family, obeying his parents totally and worshipping his ancestors, and she was expected to provide him with children, especially sons.

Mother and children playing in a garden. An 18th-century A.D. hanging scroll.

Divorce

103

A man could divorce his wife for practically anything in ancient China, even talking too much. However, he couldn't divorce her if she had no family home to which she could return.

A papyrus marriage contract from Egypt, 172 B.C.

104

In ancient Sumer, a man could divorce his wife or take another wife if the first wife didn't have any children. Children could also be adopted.

105

A divorced wife in ancient Egypt was entitled to some support from her ex-husband, no matter what the circumstances were. This support was sometimes laid down in a contract when the marriage took place, and could be as much as a third of the marriage settlement.

Work

106

Children as young as seven were given adult tasks in ancient China. Tasks included helping their parents to grow food and support the family.

107

The birth of a girl to a poor family in ancient China was full of worry. The family would have to find the money to feed her, then find her dowry (a payment to her husband's family when she got married). To help earn money, Chinese girls learned how to weave and spin cloth.

108

Girls in ancient Egypt learned how to look after the home. Boys worked in the fields with their fathers.

109

Aztec boys were taught trades by their fathers, often when they were very young. They could be sent out fishing on their own from about the age of 14.

110

The best job for a boy in Egypt was to become a government scribe. Egyptian parents wanted this for their sons more than anything else because it gave them the most influence and wealth.

A statue of an Egyptian scribe with his papyrus across his knees. Around 750 B.C.

111

Aztec girls were taught how to do household tasks such as weaving or sweeping the floor by their mothers and aunts.

Girls sweeping and learning to weave. Pictures from an Aztec book.

112

In the ancient Greek city-state of Sparta, boys had to leave their families at the age of seven and join the army to start their long, tough training to become warriors.

A bronze figure of a fierce Spartan warrior.

School

113 SIX SCHOOL SUBJECTS

studied by boys in Athens

READING
WRITING
MEMORIZING THE WORKS OF HOMER
PLAYING THE LYRE
SINGING
FITNESS AND GYMNASTICS

Boy learning to ride a horse, shown on a Greek pot.

114

Only rich Roman boys went to school. As well as reading and writing, they also learned how to be good soldiers. Schools were very strict and pupils were often beaten when they didn't behave properly.

115

Only boys from some rich families went to school in ancient Egypt. The first thing they learned was how to write government documents. They spent hours copying long, tedious lists.

Clay tablet with schoolwork, Old Babylonian, about 1900–1700 B.C.

116

All boys from rich families went to school in ancient Babylon. They learned how to write cuneiform script, starting with how to make clay tablets to write on.

117

Education was highly prized in ancient China. Chinese civil servants had to write a poem to qualify for the job. Literary exams for the civil service started in the Han Dynasty (206 B.C.– 220 A.D.).

An official writing in his study.

118

Aztec boys from ordinary families went to "houses of youth," schools where they learned skills such as carpentry, fishing, or weaving. The children of the nobility were taught in schools run by priests. The boys learned astronomy, math, architecture, and history. The priests made the boys work very hard in these "houses of tears."

Boy learning to fish, from an Aztec book.

Keeping clean

119

Most Aztec homes had their own bathhouse, called a *temazcall*, which was a little like a modern sauna. The whole family used this every day.

120

The ancient Egyptians took cleanliness seriously. To wash themselves and their clothes, they went to the river. Only the very rich had bathrooms and toilets.

121

The Greeks had no toilets at home. Instead they used chamber pots.

122

Most Romans went to public bathhouses every day to wash. These were very sociable places where people would meet with their friends.

123

The Anglo-Saxons had surprisingly good teeth because there was no sugar in their diet. Cures for toothache were based on herbs. They also used charms and amulets.

124

To get clean after exercise, ancient Greek athletes smeared olive oil on themselves, then scraped it off with a scraper called a *strigil*, bringing the dirt away with it.

Bronze figure of a boy using a strigil.

Teeth

125

Some Roman toothpaste recipes included human urine.

126

The ancient Egyptians did not have toothbrushes, but grit and straw in their bread acted as a toothbrush. As a result, the Egyptians generally had very few cavities. A bigger problem was that, because of the natural toothbrush in their bread, their teeth wore down, sometimes so quickly that they became infected. This was very painful, and could even kill.

Fashion

127

The Celts (who lived in western Europe from around 700 B.C.) used the plants around them to dye their clothes different colors. These included:

> birch bark (brown)
> goosegrass root (red and orange)
> berries (blues and purples)

128

One Anglo–Saxon monk described well-off women's fashions: they wore colorful tunics, with silk borders on the sleeves and headdresses, and red leather shoes. They had long veils on their heads; they curled their hair, and sharpened their fingernails like hawk's claws.
Do you think he approved?

129

Viking helmets didn't have horns on them! Neither did those of the Celtic peoples as a rule, although one unusual horned Celtic helmet has been found in the river Thames.

Iron Age helmet found in River Thames, London, England, 150–50 B.C.

130

Silk is a beautiful, light, shimmering material that has been made in China for about 6,000 years. The silk travelled thousands of miles along the "Silk Road" (a network of roads and sea routes) to reach Europe. It wasn't until the 6th century A.D. that European spies discovered that silk was made from the cocoons of silkworm moths.

131

Many Chinese scholars would grow their fingernails long to show that they were too clever and scholarly to do manual work. Some would leave just one fingernail long. The empress dowager Ci Xi (1835–1908 A.D.) grew each fingernail to about twice as long as her hands.

Chinese lady in flowing silk clothes, with a phoenix, painted on a silk hanging scroll. Ming Dynasty.

132

The Ainu people of the island of Hokkaido, Japan, used to weave clothes out of bark. The men would collect the bark from young trees, soften it in water, separate out the fibers, and dry it in the sun. The women would then weave it into clothes.

133

Folding fans were invented in Japan in the fourth century A.D.

Woodblock print of a Japanese actor holding a folding fan.

134

The Maya of Mexico wore clothes woven from cotton and then dyed. Other body ornaments, such as headdresses, could be made from fibers softened from the bark of trees.

135

A *quechquemitl* was a simple neck cape worn by Mexican women. Triangular in shape, sometimes decorated with tassels, nothing like it can be found anywhere else in the world.

The Aztec goddess Chalchiuhtlicue wears a *quechquemitl*.

136

Children in ancient Egypt sometimes wore no clothes at all because it was so hot. Most of the time they wore simple tunics.

137

Only Roman citizens were allowed to wear the toga. A toga was basically a large blanket shaped like a semicircle. This was draped over one arm, leaving the other one free. It must have been quite cumbersome to wear.

138

In ancient Egypt, people wore sandals made from papyrus (a kind of reed). Only rich people could afford leather sandals.

139 HOW TO DRESS IN A TOGA

1 Hold the toga behind you. Hook one pointed end over your shoulder so that it hangs down in front of you to the ground.

2 Take the other pointed end, bring it around loosely in front of you and put it over the same shoulder, tucking it in firmly behind.

3 Drape the other end over your arm.

4 Strut around looking important.

Bronze statuette of a Roman *lictor*, or *magistrate*, wearing a toga.

Papyrus sandals.

Child's leather sandals from Thebes, Egypt, 1550–1069 B.C.

140

Ancient Romans had many different types of shoes. Soldiers wore sturdy sandals with hobnails hammered into the soles to make them stronger. Workmen wore tough shoes. Richer people had beautiful slippers specially made for them.

141

Ancient Egyptian men and women wore loincloths as underwear. King Tutankhamun had 145 loincloths buried with him in his tomb, to wear during his eternal afterlife.

142

The ancient Greeks wore clothes made mainly of linen (made from fibers of the flax plant) and of wool.

143

Greek women often wore *peploi*. A *peplos* was a long piece of material folded in two and pinned together at the shoulders. It was tied around the waist with a belt.

Jewelry

144

Amazing objects made of sheets of gold have been found near the capital of the ol kingdom of Silla in Korea. Gold crowns, belts, earrings, necklaces, vessels, and even golden shoes have been excavated.

Pair of Silla dynasty gold earrings from Korea, 5th–6th centuries A.D.

147

Aztecs wore ornaments made of pottery, obsidian, and gold in pierced ears, noses, and lips.

148

The Celts from Iron Age Britain were among the most skillful metalworkers in the ancient world. They made necklaces called *torcs*, often made of several strands of metal twisted together. These could be very heavy—the gold Great Torc found at Snettisham weighs more than two pounds (over a kilogram). No wonder, because it is made from 64 separate threads.

145

The Anglo–Saxons used brooches to fasten clothes because they had no buttons. Clothes did not fit as closely then as they do now, and they had to last longer, so brooches were needed to stop them from falling off.

146

Wealthy Anglo–Saxon women wore beautiful jewelry. They especially liked using red stones called garnets and were famous for a highly skilled technique called garnet cloisonné, in which red garnets were placed into a delicate mesh of gold threads.

Great Torc from Snettisham, Norfolk, England, about 100 B.C.

Hair and headdresses

149

Women in ancient Sumer grew their hair into one long plait, which was then wound around the head. They wore beautiful headdresses of ribbons and beads, attached with pins.

150

Until they reached puberty at around 12 or 14, Egyptian children had shaved heads with just one plait of hair behind the ear. This was called a "sidelock of youth" or "Horus lock," after the god Horus, who is often shown as a child.

Hair conditioners and setting lotion were used by ancient Egyptians. Wealthy men and women wore wigs. In paintings, these are heavy and black, but some surviving wigs show they were also made in lighter colors.

152

Aztec nobles wore big headdresses made of colored feathers and other precious materials, according to their rank or status.

Wig made of human hair, from Thebes, Egypt, 1550–1300 B.C.

Some different hairstyles worn by women in ancient Greece.

153

Greek women wore their hair long and tied up. Only female slaves and those in mourning had short hair.

154

The emperor Hadrian (ruled 117–38 A.D.) started the Roman fashion for beards in the second century A.D. Until then, beards had not been popular at all with Romans, although Greek men wore them.

Marble bust of Hadrian, with a beard.

155

Chinese ladies wore elaborate high hairstyles, using false hair and held in place by pins and combs of jade, gold, silver, glass, and ivory.

Finely dressed lady with high hairdo, from a 9th-century A.D. hanging scroll.

Makeup

156

Egyptian men and women wore black or green eye makeup, and the women also used red iron oxide to color their cheeks, lips, and nails.

157

Egyptians used cleansing creams and deodorants, and rubbed on perfumed oil to protect their skin from the sun.

158

Ancient Greek face whitener was made with lead and vinegar—very bad for the skin!

An Egyptian lady's makeup.

This makeup box belonging to Ahmose of Peniati contained black kohl for the eyes, from Thebes, Egypt, 1500–1440 B.C.

159

Anglo–Saxons used to pluck out unwanted hair with metal tweezers.

Anglo–Saxon tweezers.

Food and drink

160

All the tea that we drink today comes from teas first grown and drunk in ancient China. Tea *(cha)* was drunk by rich and poor, and unusual kinds were tasted in teahouses, a popular place to meet with friends.

Jizhou tea bowl from China, 960–1279 A.D.

161

Because pomegranates are full to bursting with so many seeds, in ancient China they symbolized a good luck wish for the birth of many sons.

A Roman model of a man plowing with oxen.

162

Poor Romans ate bread, cheese, olives, beans, vegetables, and cheap meats made into pies and sausages. The emperor gave many people who lived in the big cities free handouts of bread, olive oil, and pork to eat because they were so poor (see Towns and architecture).

46

163

Three meals a day, eaten by all Romans, rich or poor:

Breakfast: *ientaculum* (children often bought breakfast from a snack bar on the way to school)

Lunch: *prandium*

Dinner: *cena*

164

In the ancient Roman world, meat was either roasted or boiled. All meat was served with rich sauces, nearly all of which contained *garum* (also called *liquamen*). This was a sauce made from the intestines, heads, and tails of fish, left out to become liquified in the sun. It sounds disgusting but actually is supposed to have tasted quite good, a little like Worcestershire sauce.

A Roman mosaic showing fish and fruit.

165

MENU FOR A RICH ROMAN'S DINNER PARTY

GUSTATIO *(appetizers)*
Eggs
Cheese
Snails fed on milk
Fish
Salad
Vegetables: asparagus, mushrooms, peas, beans, cabbage, carrots
Goose
Chicken

MENSAE PRIMAE *(main course)*
Ham
Venison
Wild boar
Goat
Hare
Ostrich
Flamingo
Parrot (served with honey, dates, and sesame seeds)

SECUNDAE MENSAE *(dessert)*
Spiced cake
Egg custard
Pastries (flavored with wine and honey)
Fruit: apples, plums, peaches, pears, grapes, figs, cherries

166

People ate bread with every meal in ancient Greece. Greeks ate fish and shellfish, but not much meat. Sheep were kept for wool and milk, but they were very rarely eaten because they were too valuable. Honey was used as a sweetener because there was no sugar.

Loaf of bread—probably a bit stale by now!— from Thebes, Egypt, around 1500 B.C.

167

In ancient Egypt, the favorite food was bread and the favorite drink was beer. People drank more beer than water.

Model of an Egyptian brewery, where the female workers are busy grinding grain and making it into beer.

Ancient Egyptians bred ducks, geese, and pigeons to eat, fattening them up on a diet of fat pellets. They also ate a lot of fish caught from the Nile as well as from lakes and marshes. Only the very wealthy ate beef, because it was extremely expensive.

Cattle painted on the wall of the tomb-chapel of Nebamun.

169

There were no potatoes or tomatoes in ancient Egypt, Greece, or Rome. Potatoes and tomatoes were two of the plants that came from the Americas. Other foods that were introduced to Europe from Mexico included chocolate, maize (a type of corn), green peppers, chili peppers, avocadoes, squash, vanilla, turkey, and chewing gum.

170

Lemons were brought to Italy by Arab traders about the 2nd century A.D. They came from the Himalayan area of northeast India. Oranges from Burma and southwest China, brought westward by Arab traders, probably reached Europe about the 9th century A.D. So Egyptians, Greeks, and Romans wouldn't have known these fruits.

**The Mayan maize god,
from Honduras, 600–800 A.D.**

171

Maize (sweet corn) was the main food of the Aztecs and Maya of ancient Mexico. It was ground between stones to make flour, which was then made into flat *tortillas* (thin pancakes). These were cooked over a hot fire and served with chili and beans. Maize was so important that maize gods were worshipped. The Maya believed that the gods made the first humans from ears of corn.

172

Chocolate, made from cacao beans, was widely used by the Maya and Aztecs and then later introduced to Europe. The Aztecs drank their *chocolatl* bitter and flavored with chilis, and they thought it provided energy and wisdom. They also used cacao beans as money.

173

Vikings used the resin from pine trees as a kind of chewing gum.

174

An Anglo–Saxon shopping list for a feast given by the king of Wessex:

> 10 jars of honey
> 20 hens
> 300 loaves of bread
> 12 casks of Welsh ale
> 1 cask of butter
> 30 casks of clear ale
> 5 salmon
> 2 old oxen
> 20 pounds' weight of hay
> 10 geese

How many people do you think were invited?

175

In Anglo–Saxon England, people drank ale from large drinking horns which were passed around a group of people. The curved shape of the horns meant that they could not be put down until they were empty. Feasts were often somewhat drunken occasions!

Anglo–Saxon drinking horn from Taplow, Buckinghamshire, England, late 6th century A.D.

An Anglo–Saxon feast.

Having fun

Music, dance, theater

176 The first professional musicians came from ancient Sumer in the third millennium B.C.

177 Dances to ensure good harvests or success in hunting were performed by the ancient Maya of Mexico.

Wooden slit-drum, or *teponaztli*, from Aztec Mexico, 1325–1521 A.D.

178 The Aztecs had many different types of instruments, including trumpets, flutes, and drums.

179

FIVE INSTRUMENTS played in ancient Sumer:

HARPS
LYRES
DRUMS

PIPES
TAMBOURINES

The queen's lyre from Ur, about 2600–2400 B.C.

180

FOUR THEATER WORDS
that we get from the ancient Greeks

Scene (*skene*): the background

Chorus: group of performers

Orchestra: large area where the chorus sang and danced

Proscenium (*proskenion*): frame around the stage

**Greek figure of an actor from
Myrina, western Asia Minor
(modern Turkey), 2nd century B.C.**

181

Beowulf is a famous Anglo–Saxon poem. It tells the story of how the "grim and greedy" monster Grendel raided the king's hall at night, killing many warriors. Beowulf the warrior killed the monster, but the next night Grendel's terrifying mother came looking for vengeance. Beowulf pursued her to her lair in the lake and killed her with his magic sword.

182

The *Book of Songs* is probably the oldest record of pop music to be found anywhere in the world. It was compiled by the *Yue-fu*, a group sent around the country by the emperor of China in 120 B.C. to report on which songs were popular.

183 Greek poetry readings were always accompanied by music. The Greeks liked to combine poetry with learning, and this could lead to some rather odd verses—for example, the poet Nicander left a set of poems listing antidotes to poison and explaining how to cure animal bites.

184 Theaters first appeared in ancient Greece. Women were not allowed to perform, so all the parts were played by men.

Orpheus playing his instrument.

185 In Greek myth, Orpheus sang and played so beautifully that his music could even tame wild beasts.

186

Many Roman plays were borrowed from ancient Greece. Other plays, based on native Roman humor, could get extremely rowdy, with actors and the audience shouting at each other during performances.

Actors in Greek comedies wore masks and padded costumes.

Toys and games

187 Children in ancient Greece played on swings and seesaws.

Children played with rag dolls with real hair in ancient Egypt. Archaeologists have found model soldiers, houses, and wooden animals in Egyptian tombs, but they may not be toys. The models may have been for the use of the dead person in the afterlife.

Wooden cat with moving mouth from Egypt, 1550–1070 B.C.

189 A team game of leapfrog called *khuzza lawizza* was played by ancient Egyptian children.

190 *Patolli* was a popular Aztec board game. Players raced their markers around a board painted on a mat. Beans marked with dots were used as dice.

An Aztec *patolli* board would have looked like this.

191 Chess is the most successful board game ever invented. It probably began in India well over 1,000 years ago. The rules have changed slightly. Originally, the queen used to be male and was called the councillor, and could not move very far.

192 Mancala is an ancient game, still very popular today across Africa and the Caribbean. There are many versions, but they all involve players "sowing" seeds or stones into rows of holes and trying to capture their opponent's pieces. It can be played extremely fast and furiously.

193

Pachisi board and pieces from Sri Lanka, 19th century.

Ludo—you have probably played it yourself—was brought to Britain in the 19th century A.D. It is based on *pachisi*, a much older game which has been popular in India for hundreds of years. Ludo is a simplified version, and is easier to play!

A mancala board from Sierra Leone, 20th century A.D.

194

The ancient Egyptians loved playing board games. The most popular was called *senet*. A number of counters had to be moved around and off the board, a little like modern backgammon. *Senet* was also played for religious reasons; it was supposed to mirror the journey taken by the soul through the afterlife.

Ivory *senet* board, with a drawer underneath to hold the pieces. Made between 1550 and 1069 B.C.

195

The Anglo-Saxons probably played a game called *tabula*, which was like backgammon. They also enjoyed playing *latrunculi* (soldiers), a game where you tried to capture your opponent's army.

196

Young women and children in ancient Greece played *astragaloi*, or knucklebones. Today we call the game "jacks." The pieces were the anklebones of sheep or goats, or pottery models of them.

197

Romans played a version of backgammon called *duodecim scriptorum*. Rude messages between opponents have been found written on the boards! For example:

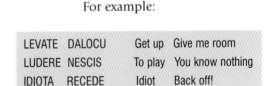

LEVATE	DALOCU		Get up	Give me room
LUDERE	NESCIS		To play	You know nothing
IDIOTA	RECEDE		Idiot	Back off!

Two women playing knucklebones. A small statue from the Hellenistic Period.

198 One of the oldest surviving board games in the world is the Royal Game of Ur. A version of this has been found scratched out next to the feet of the huge stone winged bull which guarded the gates of the city of Khorsabad. Perhaps the gate guards got bored and started a game.

199 One popular early use of kites across Asia was for fighting. Fighting kites were mostly small flat paper kites that were very agile. Part of their flying line was very rough, and this would be flown across an opponent's line to cut it and bring the kite down.

The Royal Game of Ur from Ur in Mesopotamia, 2600–2400 B.C.

200 Kites were probably invented in China. Their first mention is in a 2,000-year-old story. One version tells how a tiny general called Han Xin (who died in 196 B.C.) tied himself to a kite and flew over the emperor's palace.

Kites were originally used often for military purposes, such as to measure distance. A more likely version of Han Xin's story is that he flew the kite (without being attached to it) over the palace and marked the length of the string. He then dug a tunnel to exactly the same length under the palace walls and launched a surprise attack.

Art

201

There were many statues of emperors and gods in Roman towns and temples. Those that have survived are of white marble. When they were made they would actually have been painted in very bright colors—it's just that all the paint has worn off.

202

A bright blue paint known as Maya blue was used by the Maya of ancient Mexico in their wall paintings. How this beautiful color was made was a secret for thousands of years. Experts now think it was a mixture of indigo, clay, and tiny metal particles that make the color brighter.

203

The Nazca people of Peru lived between 200 B.C.–600 A.D. They created the mysterious Nazca lines, giant drawings on the desert floor of animals and geometric shapes. Some are over 300 feet (100 m) long and can only be seen properly from the air.

204

When the famous *discobolus* (discus thrower) sculpture in the British Museum was restored, the head was put on backwards—it should be facing back toward the discus! Ancient Greek sculptors liked to give their statues the most perfect bodies possible.

Discobolus from Hadrian's villa in Lazio, Italy, Roman copy of a Greek bronze statue, 5th century B.C.

Inventions

The calendar

205

In ancient Rome the number of months in a year = 10

This division of a year was said to be invented by Romulus, the founder of Rome, in 753 B.C. It was based on the Greek calendar, which followed the phases of the moon.

206

Days in a year = 365

The Roman emperor Julius Caesar proclaimed in 45 B.C. that from that time onward there would be 365 days in a year, with an extra day in February every four years (a leap year).

Bust of Julius Caesar, from what is now Turkey. 50 A.D.

207

The Romans counted dates inclusively, which means they counted the day they started on as one, not zero. So 2–5 September would have been four days for the Romans. This can make calculating dates in Roman documents very difficult! It also meant that, after Julius Caesar reformed the calendar, the Roman government added a leap year every three years instead of every four years. It took 36 years before the emperor Augustus finally ironed this out!

208

Months in a year after Julius Caesar revised the calendar = 12
These kept their old names:

IANUARIUS
FEBRUARIUS
MARTIUS
APRILIS
MAIUS
IUNIUS
QUINTILIS (later became "Iulius," named after Julius Caesar)
SEXTILIS (later became "Augustus," named after the Emperor Augustus)
SEPTEMBER
OCTOBER
NOVEMBER
DECEMBER

209

Months in a year after they were renamed by the emperor Charlemagne (747–814 A.D.) =12
Charlemagne renamed all of the months in Old German to describe the farming year. Starting from modern January, they are:

Wintarmanoth (winter month)
Hornung (spring)
Lentzinmanoth (Lent month)
Ostarmanoth (Easter month)
Winnemanoth (grazing month)
Brachmanoth (plowing month)
Heuvimanoth (hay month)
Aranmanoth (harvest month)
Witumanoth (wood month)
Windumemanoth (vintage month)
Herbistmanoth (autumn/harvest month)
Heilagmanoth (holy month)

210

Anglo–Saxon months of the year = 10
Starting from modern January, they are:

Solomnath (month of cakes; offerings were made to the gods)
Hrethmonath (month of the goddess Hretha)
Eosturmonath (month of the goddess Eostre; this was around the same time as Easter—we have taken the festival directly from the Anglo-Saxons)
Thirmilci (month in spring when cows are milked three times a day because the grass is lush)
Litha (month of the moon, around midsummer)
Weodmonath (month of weeds)
Haligmoanath (holy month; this is when harvest festivals were held, in late summer and early autumn)
Wintirfyllith (the first full moon of winter)
Blotmonath (blood month, the month when animals had to be killed for winter food)
Giuli (yuletide; this lasted for two months, including the winter solstice festival)

211

Days of the week = 7 (with their Roman and Anglo–Saxon pagan roots)

SUNDAY (day of the sun)
MONDAY (day of the moon)
TUESDAY (Tiw's day; Tiw was the god of war)
WEDNESDAY (Woden's day; Wodin was chief of the gods)
THURSDAY (Thor's day; Thor was god of thunder)
FRIDAY (Freya's day; Freya was the wife of Woden)
SATURDAY (Saturn's day; Saturn was the Roman god of agriculture)

212

The Anglo-Saxons considered the new day to begin at sunset on the previous one. Therefore, the time after sunset Saturday would actually be called *Sunnanniht* (Sunday night), becoming *Sunnandæg* (Sun day) with the sunrise.

213

The ancient Egyptians had a 10-hour day for practical purposes, although in some texts they described a 24-hour day. They had clocks, including sand and water clocks, to help them tell time.

214

The Aztecs had two calendars, one for living and working by, the other for religious rituals. Each day was ruled over by a god. A giant image of the calendar was carved on a big stone in the central square of the capital Tenochtitlan. The calendar was also recorded on folding books made of deerskin.

215

The Egyptians thought that some days were lucky and others unlucky, and they consulted a calendar like the one on this papyrus to check before they planned anything. The bad days are written in red hieroglyphs. An example of a bad day: "Do not go out on this day . . . whoever is born on this day will die through a serpent."

Egyptian papyrus with a calendar of lucky and unlucky days, around 1225 B.C.

216

Signs of the zodiac = 12

It was probably the Babylonian astrologers in the first millennium B.C. who thought of dividing the year into the 12 signs of the zodiac, based on star constellations they could see in the sky. How the sun moved through these was used to predict what would happen on Earth. The signs as we know them today are taken from their ancient Latin names.

217

Ophiuchus (the serpent-bearer) is actually the thirteenth constellation that the sun passes through during the year. It comes after Scorpio and before Sagittarius. However, it does not have a sign of the zodiac to go with it.

218

The Mayan calendar was based on observing the stars and doing basic mathematical calculations. It was astonishingly accurate. The Maya worked out the cycle of Venus for over 6,000 years with only one day's error!

The signs of the zodiac are:

ARIES (ram)

TAURUS (bull)

GEMINI (twins)

CANCER (crab)

LEO (lion)

VIRGO (maiden)

LIBRA (scales)

SCORPIO (scorpion)

SAGITTARIUS (archer)

CAPRICORN (goat)

AQUARIUS (water-bearer)

PISCES (fish)

THE TWELVE ANIMALS
of the Chinese zodiac

219

GOAT MONKEY

HORSE ROOSTER

SNAKE DOG

DRAGON PIG

RABBIT RAT

TIGER OX

Transport

220

The Aztecs had no vehicles with wheels at all—they just had wheels on a few toys.

221

The Aztecs had no pack animals. Loads were carried by the people themselves, or their slaves if they were lucky. The Aztecs were amazed to see the Spanish invaders riding horses.

222

The ancient Maya, like the Aztecs, did not have wheeled vehicles and so they walked everywhere. Rich nobles were carried around in litters, and traders also made journeys by canoe.

223

The Maya had an extensive road system linking their cities; it was also used for processions and journeys to special religious places.

Model of a boat from ancient Egypt, about 1900 B.C.

224

Viking longship.

225

Egyptians often traveled by boat. The river Nile flowed south to north, so they rowed in this direction. To come back, they hoisted a sail to take advantage of the wind blowing north to south.

The Vikings traveled in longships. These were double-ended craft built of overlapping planks with a single square sail. They were very sturdy in rough seas. The sailors kept their possessions in trunks and sat on them to row. The Vikings gave their ships names such as *Strider, Crane, Long Serpent,* or *Bison.*

226

In ancient Greece most people walked to get around. Carriages and horses were only for the rich. Peasants might own a donkey.

228

The ancient Egyptians mostly used donkeys for transportation. Horses were only used by the very rich. Camels were not used until late in Egyptian history.

227

Most cargo in ancient Greece (such as oil or wine) was carried in large pottery jars called *amphorae*. Cargo often went by ship around the coast of Greece or between the islands.

In the middle of this Greek cup a man is lifting an *amphora*. Cargo ships sail around the edge of the cup.

229

There were only a few paved roads in ancient Greece. Most roads were just rough tracks.

230

To get from town to town, most Romans used covered wagons or carts. They were covered in cloth with seats on top. They were bumpy, slow, and very uncomfortable.

231

Roman roads "cut through mountains and eliminated the bends," as it said on a Roman milestone in Germany. They were the best roads ever seen.

232

Corn from Egypt arrived in the Roman Empire on huge boats, the supertankers of the ancient world.

Technology

233

Tool making began in East Africa about 2.4 million years ago. Early humans began to shape the tools they needed, instead of just picking up sticks or sharp-edged stones. They discovered that by using a hard stone as a hammer, they could knock flakes off both sides of a pebble to create sharp edges. These tools could be used to chop branches from trees or cut meat from large animal carcasses.

Paleolithic stone-chopping tools from Tanzania, Africa, about 1.8 million years old.

234

Water clocks were invented thousands of years ago in China. They started out as a series of jars that would each empty after a set time.

235

During the Tang Dynasty (618–907 A.D.) in China, canals were built to bring water to distant areas to help grow rice, the main crop. The water was brought up to the fields by an ingenious chain-and-paddle system operated by turning a crank.

Rice fields in China. This watercolor was painted in China in the 19th century for export to Europe.

236

The Great Wall of China was built in the 3rd century B.C., on the orders of Zheng of the Qin, the First Emperor of China, as a defense against invading tribes. It was an amazing 4,000 miles (6,000 km) long. Watchtowers were built every few hundred yards. The wall we see today was heavily restored during the Ming dynasty (1368–1644 A.D.).

237

The Chinese discovered how to make porcelain in the 6th century A.D., more than 1,000 years before the Europeans managed to invent it. It was in huge demand in Europe, and enormous amounts were imported from China.

Porcelain flask made in China for export to Spain, 1573–1620 A.D.

TEN THINGS
THAT THE ROMANS DID FOR US

The Romans had by far the most advanced technology of their times. Many Roman inventions and introductions were lost after the downfall of the Roman Empire, and were not rediscovered for many centuries.

238 Lighthouses at the entrances to many harbors. Egyptians and Greeks first used lighthouses, and the Romans brought them to Britain (you can see the remains of one at Dover).

239 Enormous cranes to help with construction work, powered by slaves walking inside huge wheels.

240 Glass-blowing meant glass could be mass-produced, so one no longer had to be very rich to afford it.

Blown glass jug from Roman Britain, 2nd century A.D.

241 Plumbing: the Romans invented aqueducts and lead pipes for transporting water. They built the longest known tunnel of the time—3.5 miles (5.6 km) long—to drain a lake.

242 Concrete: the strength and lightness of Roman concrete made possible great domes, bridges, arches, and aqueducts that could not have been built from stone. The Romans also knew that adding horsehair made concrete less likely to shrink, and adding blood made it resistant to frost.

243 Transport: Roman roads were used for up to a thousand years after the empire fell. At their peak they covered a total of 53,000 miles (85,000 km). Changing stations could enable a courier to cover nearly 500 miles (800 km) in 24 hours using relays of horses.

244 Central heating: the Romans used a clever system of underfloor heating, called the *hypocaust*, to heat rooms in the public baths and in the villas of wealthy people.

245 Farming: harvesting machines invented by the Romans were not improved upon until the 19th century A.D.

246 Math: the abacus, probably invented in Mesopotamia, was the first portable counting machine ever. The Romans introduced it to Britain.

247 Architecture: the Roman arch was perfected, and the impressive roof dome was invented.

Medicine and illness

248

The oldest prescriptions in the world, dating from about 3000 B.C., have been found on a clay tablet from ancient Sumer. They explain how to make a poultice for a wound from parts of plants crushed together with oil, and how to make medicines from natural ingredients such as shells, beer, plants, salt, and ashes.

249

The people of Sumer thought that most of the causes of illness were supernatural and were the result of curses, the will of a god, or witchcraft.

They had two types of doctors: the *asuu*, who administered practical remedies; and the *ashipu*, a magician who used spells. These would often work together to try to cure a patient.

250

The Greek Hippocrates is known as the father of modern medicine. He was the first person to observe the patient carefully and try to come up with a diagnosis without being influenced by superstition. He is probably the most famous doctor of all time. Some modern doctors still take the Hippocratic Oath to "first do no harm," named after him.

251

Many of the ancient Greeks believed that you could only be well if you had the right balance of the four "humors" in your body. The humors were:

- black bile
- yellow bile
- blood
- phlegm

For this reason, doctors often advised vomiting or bloodletting to restore the body's balance.

A Greek doctor examines a boy with a swollen stomach. On the right is a cupping vessel, used to draw blood or pus. The vessel is much larger than it would be in real life.

252

Asklepios was the doctor god of ancient Greece. A cult grew up around him. Patients slept in his temples, hoping to be sent a dream that would tell them what would cure them.

Marble head of Asklepios.

253

The ancient Egyptians liked using dung to treat a whole range of illnesses. This included the dung of crocodiles, pelicans, and lizards. They even used human feces for some ailments.

254

The Babylonians thought that toothache was caused by a worm.

73

255

Hoping to be cured, Greeks and Romans left carved models of their afflicted body parts in temples dedicated to Asklepios. Large numbers of model legs, feet, arms, eyes, and ears have been found.

Terracotta models of an eye and ear.

A thank-you to Asklepios for making a leg better, left in a temple on the island of Milos, Greece, 100–200 A.D.

256

Tuberculosis was around in ancient Egyptian times. It was caught from drinking milk or eating meat from infected cows, and showed up in damage to the spine. This can be seen in some Egyptian mummies.

257

Between 430 and 426 B.C., Athens suffered outbreaks of a terrible plague, which killed almost a third of the population.

Symptoms included:
SHAKING, SORES AND ULCERS COVERING THE BODY, VOMITING, A BLEEDING MOUTH AND THROAT, AND THEN DEATH.

The plague was probably brought in from northern Africa on overcrowded boats.

258

The ancient Egyptians had remedies for common health problems. One cure for a skin complaint contained aloe vera (a plant which we still use today for the skin), cucumber, and wine. Pigs' teeth and tortoise bile were used in other remedies. However, Egyptians thought that these would only work if used with the right magic spells.

259

The perfectly preserved body of a head louse was found in the hair of an Egyptian who died 5,000 years ago. Remedies of oily lotions to get rid of head lice are found in ancient Egyptian texts.

260

The Greek city of Cyrene (now in modern Libya) flourished because of its trade in a plant called *silphium*. As well as being used in cooking, this was used to treat many ailments including sickness, colds, and headaches. *Silphium* is sadly now extinct, so we cannot test it for ourselves.

Silver coin from Cyrene showing a *silphium* plant.

261

Viking men and women had long hair. Combs were probably used to remove head lice as well as to make hair look tidy.

263

Dung was used to cure a large number of ailments in ancient Rome. The Roman writer Pliny listed a whole range of dung treatments, including eating mouse feces to sweeten bad breath.

262

Doctors in ancient Rome were able to amputate arms and legs, and set bones. They learned a great deal about surgery from the Egyptians and the Greeks. Archeologists have found many beautifully crafted surgical instruments from Rome.

A set of Roman surgical instruments.

264

Some oculists (eye doctor specialists) in ancient Rome could operate on such problems as in-growing eyelashes. This was without anesthetic (not invented until the 19th century A.D.), and without proper cleanliness, so many patients died.

265

Anglo–Saxons thought that eating goat's fat was a good treatment for dysentery.

266

The later Anglo–Saxons believed that wine, sometimes warmed up or spiced, had medicinal qualities.

267

In ancient China, people believed that sickness was brought on by an evil wind. They wore charms and amulets to ward off the bad spirits that caused this, or even had the spirits exorcised.

268

The legendary Emperor Shennang (ruled about 5,000 years ago) was known as the father of Chinese agriculture. He is believed to have written 365 herbal, mineral, and animal remedies in a manual. Some of these are still used today, such as rhubarb, which helps relieve constipation.

Eye doctor's stamp used for marking ointments, from Roman Britain, 1st–4th century A.D.

269

It was considered incredibly rude for male doctors to touch female patients in ancient China, so instead they used dolls on which the patient could point out which part was hurting.

270

Acupuncture was invented in China, and has been practiced from about 2700 B.C. to today. It is based on the theory that energy moves through the body and can be rebalanced, using needles inserted into the correct pathways.

271

Buddhist monks in India had to carry five simple medicines wherever they went, including fresh butter, molasses, and honey.

272

Cutting off the nose was a punishment in ancient India. Doctors figured out how to rebuild noses using skin cut from the cheek, with tubes of reeds to keep the nostrils open. This is one of the earliest known types of plastic surgery.

273

The Black Death first swept across Europe in the mid-14th century, killing between one-third and two-thirds of the population. At the same time, similar epidemics attacked Asia and the Middle East. The plague was to return frequently until the 1700s A.D., hitting London particularly hard in 1666 A.D. The most common form was the bubonic plague, where victims had large pus-filled swellings and dark blotches on their bodies. The Black Death had a huge effect on the way people thought about death, religion, and each other.

The Rich Man, **from the Dance of Death series o paintings by Holbein, shows that death does not care how much money you have. 1526 A.D.**

Rulers

EGYPTIAN PHARAOHS

274 Each Egyptian pharaoh had five official names: his own birth name and four others he chose when he took the throne. The full name of Ramesses II translates as (take a deep breath):

Strong Bull, Beloved of Maat
Protector of Egypt and Curber of Foreign Lands
Powerful of Years, Great of Successes
Powerful is the Justice of Ra
Ramesses

275 Egyptian pharaohs were sometimes named after a famous earlier king. How many Egyptian pharaohs had the same name?

Ramesses = 11
Thutmose = 4
Amenemhat = 7
Amenhotep = 4
Cleopatra = 7
Ptolemy = 15

Statue of Amenhotep III, who ruled around 1390–1352 B.C.

276

Pepi II was said to have ruled Egypt for a staggering 94 years! He was only six when he came to the throne, and was the pharaoh who ruled longest. Pepi II is believed to have ruled from 2278 to 2184 B.C. However, there is a lack of definite information about him, so we cannot be completely certain of these dates. The next contender is Ramesses II, the Great. We know he ruled for 66 years, from 1279 to 1213 B.C.

Huge stone bust of Ramesses II, made around 1250 B.C.

277

The youngest Egyptian pharaoh for whom we have definite records was Tutankhamun, who ascended the throne in 1336 B.C. at the tender age of nine. He was only 17 when he died, possibly assassinated by a blow to the back of his head.

278 Ancient China was made up of many states, often at war with one another. The country was unified for the first time in 221 B.C. when the ruthless King Zheng of Qin conquered his enemies and became the first emperor. The English name for China comes from Qin, which is pronounced "chin."

The first emperor of China.

Statue of Ashurnasirpal II, 883–859 BC.

279 The Assyrian Empire stretched across northern Mesopotamia and was powerful in the 1st millennium B.C. Ten names of Assyrian kings:

Ashuruballit
Tukulti-Ninurta
Ashur-dan
Adad-nirari
Ashurnasirpal
Tiglath-Pileser
Sargon
Sennacherib
Esarhaddon
Ashurbanipal

280

The most successful conqueror in history was probably Alexander the Great (356–323 B.C.). He was the first king of all Greece and his vast empire reached nearly to India. He only stopped his conquests when he got to India because his army refused to go any further. He trained his huge war horse, Bucephalus, when he was only nine, and rode him into several battles.

281

Marble portrait of Alexander the Great, 2nd–1st century B.C.

When Alexander, having reached India, decided to turn back westward, the Indian ruler Chandragupta (ruled 322–298 B.C.) led an army to reclaim the lands Alexander had conquered. When Chandragupta had done this, he turned to the east and conquered lands there, too. For the first time, most of India was united under one powerful ruler. Later in his life, Chandragupta gave up the throne to become a monk, and ended his days in deliberate semistarvation.

282

Genghis Khan (1162–1227 A.D.) founded the Mongolian empire, the largest empire in the history of the world. He did this by uniting all the people of the steppes into a formidable army. In spite of popular belief, he was a politician rather than a marauder. He was good at military intelligence and made careful battle plans. Genghis Khan means "Lord of the Earth." His real name was Temujin.

283

Eric Bloodaxe got his nickname when, as a young man in Norway, he murdered several of his brothers. Eric ruled the parts of England the Vikings had conquered from Jorvik (York), the Viking capital from 947–954 A.D. He often took time off from ruling to go raid and murder in Scotland and Ireland. Eric Bloodaxe was eventually killed in battle by the king of Wessex.

ROMAN
EMPERORS

284

According to legend, Romulus was the first ruler of Rome. He and his brother Remus were said to have been left in the wild by their stepfather's wicked brother, and brought up by a she-wolf.

Silver coin showing Romulus and Remus with the she-wolf, made around 275–260 B.C.

285

The most insane Roman emperor was probably Caligula (ruled 37–41 A.D.). He sailed in jewel-encrusted ships equipped as floating palaces; he drank dissolved pearls; and he even considered making his favorite racehorse a consul. Eventually, Caligula even thought himself a god. He dressed as one and demanded worship.

286

The emperor Hadrian built a huge wall across the north of Britain to keep out the fierce tribes who lived in Caledonia. The wall was manned by Roman soldiers, who must have found it very damp and cold.

287

Nero's reign (54–68 A.D.) started peacefully, but he gradually became more cruel and unpredictable. He forced people to watch him perform on stage for hours (and applaud enthusiastically), and he had thousands of people executed on a whim.

Statuette of Nero from Roman Britain, 1st century A.D.

288 THE FIRST TEN
EMPERORS OF ROME
AND HOW THEY DIED

It was very dangerous to be emperor.
Many did not die of natural causes.

AUGUSTUS: natural causes, aged 71
(but there were rumors that his wife Livia
had him poisoned)

TIBERIUS: natural causes, aged 77
(although there was a rumor that Caligula
had him smothered)

CALIGULA: murdered by his own guards,
aged 29

**Cameo portrait of Augustus,
made around 14–20 A.D.**

Bronze head of Claudius, found in Britain, 1st century A.D.

Marble head of Vespasian, made around 70–80 A.D.

CLAUDIUS: probably poisoned by his wife, Agrippina, aged 64

NERO: committed suicide after being deposed, aged 31

GALBA: ruled for only seven months before being killed, aged 72 and sick, by Otho's soldiers

OTHO: ruled for only three months before committing suicide, aged 37, after defeat by Vitellius

VITELLIUS: ruled for only eight months before being killed, aged 54, by Vespasian's troops

VESPASIAN: died of natural causes, aged 70

TITUS: died of a fever (though possibly poisoned by his doctor), aged 42

Britain

289

The legend of King Arthur comes from the time after the fall of the Roman empire when the Anglo–Saxons first invaded Britain. The later medieval story tells how the British King Arthur, helped by his knights of the Round Table and the wizard Merlin, won many battles against Saxon invaders. There are older records of a warrior called Arthur from around this time, but his name is all we know for certain. There is no mention anywhere of Merlin or the knights.

290

King Offa was the Anglo–Saxon king of Mercia (reigned 757–96 A.D.). He built Offa's Dyke, a long earthwork along the Welsh border, to keep out invaders and raiders from the west.

291

Alfred the Great, king of Wessex (reigned 871–99 A.D.) is probably the most famous Anglo–Saxon king. At the start of his reign he had to retreat from the Vikings. There is a story that when he was hiding, a woman asked him to watch her cakes on the fire, but because he was a king he didn't know how to cook and let them burn. Eventually, Alfred defeated the Vikings and ruled over most of England.

Silver penny of Alfred the Great, 871–99 A.D.

292

King Cnut was such a powerful king that his followers told him he could even stop the tide from coming in. So he went down to the beach and tried to stop the tide, possibly to show them they were wrong. Of course, he just got wet instead. But this story was first told long after Cnut died, and it probably never happened. Cnut was the first Viking to rule all of England, from 1016 to 1035 A.D. He was also king of Denmark and Norway.

Coin of King Cnut, 1016–1035 A.D.

293

Moctezuma II, the Aztec emperor (1502–20 A.D.), had to face terrible problems during his reign. These included a plague of locusts, a famine, and a flood. These were considered to be bad omens, and sure enough later in his reign the Spanish invaded, wiped out his government, and murdered thousands of his people. Moctezuma was killed in the fighting.

294

This picture sign (called a glyph) writes the name Eight Deer, with eight circles and a deer's head.

The Mixtec ruler Eight Deer was a great player of the ball game (see page 115 for more about the ball game). Sometimes the game was used to settle an argument between cities. The winning team would gain control of the city and the losing team would be sacrificed. Eight Deer won several cities in this way, until he finally lost a game—and his life.

Powerful (and frightening!) women

295

Head of a woman resembling Cleopatra, Roman, around 50–30 B.C.

Cleopatra VII (reigned 51–30 B.C.) first ruled Egypt with her half-brother Ptolemy XIII, but he drove her out. Julius Caesar, her Roman lover, helped her regain the throne. She was flamboyant and sensual, at one point dissolving a pearl in wine and drinking it. She then fought the emperor Augustus, with the help of her second Roman lover, Mark Anthony. Augustus finally defeated her in 31 B.C. It is often said that Cleopatra poisoned herself with a snakebite, but this was probably made up by writers in much later times.

296

Empress Irene: when Constantine VI became emperor of Byzantium in 780 A.D. he was still a child and his mother Irene ruled for him. When he became an adult, she did not want to give up power, and they quarrelled. In 797 A.D. Irene had Constantine blinded and imprisoned so he would not be able to rule. Constantine died from his injuries. She then became empress, the first woman to rule Byzantium in her own name.

297

Livia (58 B.C.–29 A.D.) was married to Augustus, the first Roman emperor, for over 50 years. Although she had no official position, she was a huge power behind the throne. Much of this continued after Augustus died. It was rumored that Livia had several people murdered, including Augustus himself, and his nephew and grandsons. She wanted them out of the way so that her own son Tiberius (by her first marriage) could become the next emperor.

Portrait of Wu Zetian.

298

Boudica (died 60–61 A.D.) was the ruler of the Iceni tribe in Iron Age Britain. After her husband was killed, she was very harshly treated by the Romans. She led her people in revolt against the Roman invaders, and although she was eventually defeated and killed, she managed to inflict great damage, destroying Camulodunum (Colchester), Londinium (London), and Verulamium (St. Albans), and killing thousands.

299

Of all the hundreds of rulers of ancient Egypt, there were only three female rulers who governed in their own right without being married to a king or pharaoh—Queens Sobekneferu, Hatshepsut, and Tawosret.

Gold ring with Hatshepsut's name in hieroglyphs.

300

Wu Zetian (625–705 A.D.) was the only woman to govern China in her own right in the 2,100-year history of China's emperors. She used the name Shengshen. At first she was a concubine of the emperor, and she used her beauty, cleverness, and cruelty to be made empress consort—she had the previous consort put to death horribly by having her arms and legs broken, then leaving her in a huge wine jar for several days. Eventually, when the emperor became ill, she ruled in his place.

Society

How different peoples were ruled

Aztecs

301

The Aztec emperor was completely in charge, advised by groups of nobles. Ordinary people had to do as they were told.

302

The Aztecs actually called themselves the Mexica, which is where the modern name for Mexico comes from. "Aztec" is a name that was invented for them later!

ROME

303

The emperor held most of the power in ancient Rome. He was advised by the Senate, which was a legislature voted for by the Roman citizens. Citizens could not be very poor people, foreigners, or women.

304

There were three classes of Roman citizens. It was possible to move from one class to another if you had enough money. The classes were:

PLEBEIANS (ordinary working men)

EQUITES ("knights"—fairly wealthy men but not nobles)

PATRICIANS (the aristocrats)

Roman emperors wore crowns of laurel leaves on their heads. This was because they didn't want to be seen as kings, but as military leaders.

Gold oak wreath, 350–300 B.C.

305

306

After the emperor, the most important men in Rome were the two powerful consuls, in charge of the army and the government.

307

Kings had made themselves pretty unpopular in Rome! Tarquinius Superbus, the last king of Rome, was an arrogant tyrant. The Romans threw him out in 510 B.C., and for centuries ruled themselves as a republic instead.

GREECE

Silver coin showing the goddess Athena and her owl from Athens, around 480 B.C.

308

Greece consisted of many different city–states and areas, each of which was ruled in its own way. Athens was unusual in that it became a democracy (*demos* means "people" and *kratos* means "rule") where citizens who attended the Assembly all had a vote in the running of the city. Women, foreigners, and many others were not allowed to vote.

309 Egypt

The pharaoh had a council of specially chosen men to give him advice. The Egyptians believed that the pharaoh was part divine, and acted as a link between the world of men and the gods—so his commands had to be obeyed like those of a god.

CRIME AND PUNISHMENT

310

Being sent to work in the mines was the punishment for many crimes in ancient Egypt. Other punishments included moving large blocks of stone or doing other manual labor. The Egyptians did not punish too harshly on the whole, although stealing from a royal grave got the death penalty.

311

There were police in ancient Egypt but they mainly looked after the pharaoh or king. They didn't help the public at all.

312

The worst punishment in ancient China—for example, for someone who had murdered his or her parents—was to be killed by being slowly cut to pieces.

Coin of Diocletian, early 4th century A.D.

313

The Roman emperor Diocletian (ruled 284–305 A.D.) thought Christianity was a threat to Roman society. He arrested Christians and sent them to fight wild lions in the arenas without any means of protecting themselves.

314

In medieval England, the worst crime was treason (plotting against the king). For men, this was punished with hanging, drawing, and quartering. First the victim would be dragged to the place of execution, then hanged until not quite dead, then drawn (disembowelled) with his body parts burned in front of him, and then cut into four quarters, which would be displayed in different cities around the country to discourage other people from committing the same crime.

315

When they reached the age of about 13, Spartan boys were tested by being sent out into the countryside where they had to steal in order to survive. However, if they got caught they were severely beaten.

316

Roman slaves were often treated very harshly. For example, if they tried to run away, they could be burned alive or sent to the arena to fight wild beasts.

Metal tag that was probably attached to a slave—or a dog. The writing says "Hold me if I run away and return me to my master Viventius on the estate of Callistus."

Women

317

According to Confucian custom in ancient China, men made the rules and women were supposed to obey them. A woman had to do what her parents told her, then what her husband told her, and when he died what her eldest son told her. However, in practice some women had great power over their children.

Chinese family in a garden, 18th century A.D.

318

At special occasions, such as dinner parties, Greek women were not allowed to eat with the men, but stayed in their own quarters. However, paid female entertainers might eat with the men.

319

Roman women could not vote or hold powerful office. The only job in which they could achieve rank was as a priestess. All other important posts were open to men only.

320

Greek actors were all men. Women were probably not even allowed to watch plays.

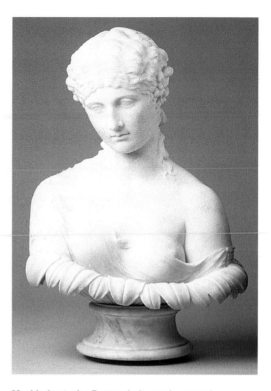

Marble bust of a Roman lady, made around 40–50 A.D.

An Egyptian model of a female servant.

321

Greek female babies could be left outside to die if their parents could not afford to keep them.

322

A woman's place in ancient Egypt was in the home. Women's skin was often colored paler than men's in wall paintings to show that they spent most of their time indoors.

The spiritual world

Religion

Pagans are people who worship a number of gods, often gods of nature. Most people in Europe were pagan before the advent of Christianity. Christians believe in one God. Christianity spread rapidly across Europe starting in late Roman and early medieval times, although many people did not abandon their pagan gods quickly or without resistance.

323

Six people in Christian prayer. This picture was painted on the wall of a Roman villa in eastern Britain.

324

King Oswald of Northumbria (633–42 A.D.) was an early Anglo–Saxon Christian king who was killed in battle by the pagan king Penda of Mercia. His head and limbs were impaled on spikes. Oswald, was later declared a saint; one description of his head says it was "... glowing a deep yellow color which surpasses the yellowness of wax and is closer in its great beauty and loveliness to the appearance of gold ..."

325

The Vikings were pagans. Odin was the chief of their gods. He carried a spear and had one eye. He had two ravens called Huginn and Muninn (thought and memory) who whispered secrets to him.

326

The Druids were important priests who
carried out religious rituals in the Iron Age
in Britain. They may have sacrificed
humans. Mistletoe pollen was found in the
stomach of Lindow Man (see page 14) and
this plant was important to Druids.

327

In Bronze and Iron Age Britain, many weapons were
thrown into water or buried in the ground, perhaps as
sacrifices (gifts) to the pagan gods. This has helped
preserve them for us to study.

**This shield was thrown into the river Thames, London,
England between 350–50 B.C.**

328

Reliquaries are containers that hold partial remains of saints, such as their teeth, fingerbones, or hair. They have been used by many religions. One silver reliquary was made in the shape of a head to keep pieces from the skull of St. Eustace. According to legend, Eustace was a Roman general who converted to Christianity and was burned to death with his family when he refused to give thanks to the Roman gods.

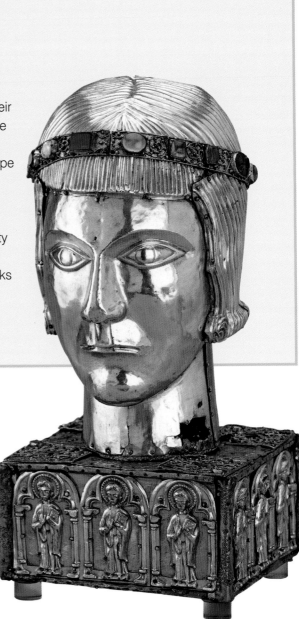

Reliquary of St. Eustace, 1210 A.D.

329 TWELVE GREEK GODS

The Greeks believed that their 12 main gods lived at the top of Mount Olympus, in northeast Greece. They were:

Zeus — king of the gods and god of the weather

Poseidon — god of the sea

Hera — wife of Zeus, goddess of marriage and of the sky and stars

Demeter — the goddess of farming and the earth

Hestia — goddess of home and family. These were brothers and sisters. The other Olympian gods were children of Zeus.

Marble statue of Demeter, carved around 350 B.C.

Bronze head of Apollo, from around 460 B.C.

Artemis — goddess of animals and the hunt and protector of young girls

Apollo — god of light, telling the future, music, medicine, and archery

Athena — goddess of wisdom, crafts, education, and war. Her symbol was the owl.

Hephaestus — the craftsman of the gods, also the god of fire, workmen, and weapons

Ares — the god of war and slaughter

Aphrodite — the goddess of love and beauty

Hermes — the messenger of the gods, also the god of travelers, trade, and inventions

330

Hades was the next most powerful god after Zeus and Poseidon, but he ruled over the underworld, and so was not on Mount Olympus.

331

Ordinary people weren't allowed inside sacred Greek temples, so the altars were put outside, where they could worship.

332

Dionysus was the god of wine, plants, and the theater. He is not always considered to be an Olympian because his mother was a mortal (a human who would die, and therefore not a god).

ROMAN GODS

333

The Romans had many different gods and goddesses ruled by Jupiter, the god of thunder and the sky. Their most important gods were shared with ancient Greece and given Roman names (such as Bacchus instead of Dionysus), and they also added extra gods from peoples they had conquered.

Bronze figure of Jupiter, 2nd century A.D. He probably once held a thunderbolt.

334

The Romans, like many other ancient peoples, believed that blood sacrifices (killing an animal) were the best way to talk to the gods. On her birthday, a Roman woman would sacrifice an animal as a present to the goddess Juno, queen of the gods. White animals, such as sheep, were often sacrificed to Jupiter, because white was his favorite color.

335

The Romans loved holding festivals to honor the gods. They had 32 festivals just in the month of January.

336

The Vestal Virgins were women who worked in the temple for the goddess Vesta, keeping a sacred fire always burning for her. Vesta was the Roman name for Hestia, Greek goddess of the hearth.

337

Roman priests and priestesses covered their heads with a veil, or a fold of the toga, when they performed sacrifices to the gods.

338

Roman figure of Bacchus holding an empty winecup, with his panther at his feet.

In places, the riotous worship of Bacchus really got out of hand. The Romans tried to ban it altogether, then were forced to regulate it and bring it more into mainstream religion.

The ancient Egyptians worshipped many gods. Most of these had animals associated with them, and could be shown with animal heads.

339 SIX EGYPTIAN ANIMAL-HEADED GODS

1 **ANUBIS**, with the head of a jackal, mummified and protected the dead.
2 **RA**, the powerful sun god, had the head of a falcon.
3 **THOTH**, with the head of an ibis (a kind of bird) or a baboon, was the scribe of the gods.
4 **HATHOR**, the daughter of Ra and goddess of music and dancing, had the head of a cow.
5 **SEKHMET**, a goddess who was a ferocious protector of Ra, had the head of a lioness.
6 **KHEPRI**, with the head of a scarab beetle, was said to push the sun through the sky.

Statue of Sekhmet.

Statue of a baboon from Egypt, 1350 B.C.

Anubis supervising the "Weighing of the Heart" ceremony, to judge if a dead person had been good or bad.

340

In ancient Egypt there were main temples for each of the gods. Here, the king and high priests performed certain rites and received offerings. Ordinary people were never allowed inside, and only saw the god's statue during special festivals when the statue was carried outside the temple.

341 SEVEN ATZEC GODS

The Aztecs believed in a huge number of gods who created and controlled the world, and kept the sun moving across the sky.

1 **Quetzalcoatl**, "feathered serpent," was the god of learning and of the wind.
2 **Tezcatlipoca**, "smoking mirror," was the god of night, sorcery, and war. He was twinned with Quetzalcoatl, whose opposite he was.
3 **Xipe Totec**, "our flayed lord," was the god of the seasons, growth, and vegetation. He is usually shown wearing a flayed (stripped) human skin.
4 **Tlaloc**, "the great provider," was god of fertility and rain.
5 **Coatlicue**, "she of the serpent skirt," was mother of the moon and stars, and goddess of women who die in childbirth.
6 **Chicomecoatl**, the goddess of ripe maize. The Aztecs had three goddesses just for the maize plant (sweetcorn), their most important crop.
7 **Chalchiuhtlicue** was the goddess of the waters, and wore a skirt the color of water.

Mosaic mask of Tezcatlipoca, based on a human skull. 15th–16th century A.D.

342

The Maya believed that in shedding their own blood they were making contact with the gods and showing that they were brave. One carving shows a queen passing a rope of thorns through her tongue and another shows her husband pricking his penis with a sharp stick.

343

The ancient Maya believed that the gods watched everything they did, and it was important to perform the right rituals every day to keep the gods happy. They had many gods and goddesses—of the stars and the sun, of rain, of maize, and of different months and days.

Maya carving from Yaxchilan, Mexico, showing the queen shedding her blood.

There were several different belief systems in ancient China. They existed side by side, and included Buddhism, Taoism, and Confucianism. Confucius (Kong Fu zi, the master Kong, 551–479 B.C.) was a Chinese philosopher who said that people should honor their families and ancestors, and that this would eventually strengthen the whole country. Today there are still many belief systems in China.

A rubbing of Confucius.

345

Muslims believe in only one God, like Christians and Jews. All three religions look to Abraham as a respected forefather. In the Muslim holy book the Qu'ran, Christians, Jews, and Muslims are called the "Children of the Book."

The beginning of the *basmala*, which starts every chapter of the Qu'ran, "In the name of Allah the merciful ..."

346

Hinduism probably comes from a much older religion found in the ancient Indus Valley in India over 4,000 years ago. Hinduism as a religion did not start until hundreds of years after the Indus Valley civilization died out, and the connection between the two remains a mystery.

347

The sacred books of Hinduism are called the *Vedas*. There are four *Vedas*. They are a collection of truths revealed by the gods. They were written down earlier than 1000 B.C., and are the only surviving records from this time. The first book is the holiest. It is called the *Rig Veda*.

348 THE THREE MOST IMPORTANT HINDU GODS

Since about 100 B.C., the three most important Hindu gods have been:

1 **Brahma**, "the Creator," a four-headed god whose fifth head was cut off by Shiva.

2 **Vishnu**, "the Preserver," has appeared in a number of incarnations in order to help mankind. Hindus say that his latest appearance was as Buddha in the 6th century A.D.

3 **Shiva**, "the Destroyer," is the most powerful god of all, who can appear in various forms.

349

The *Mahabharata* and the *Ramayana* are the two great epic poems of ancient India. They are very important to the Hindu religion. The *Mahabharata* is a collection of myths about the main Hindu gods, and the *Ramayana* is the story of Rama and Sita. It is hard to date these, but a first version of the *Ramayana* was probably written around 500–300 B.C., while the *Mahabharata* was written in the 2nd century A.D.

Statuette of Parvati, the wife of Shiva. From India, early 11th century A.D.

350

Gautama Siddhartha was born in India in about 560 B.C. He was a royal prince whose family kept him hidden away in the palace. When he was nearly 30 he finally snuck out and discovered to his horror that people could suffer and die. He decided to stop being a prince and travel the land looking for happiness and freedom from these worries. He finally achieved this and people began to call him Buddha, which means "the enlightened." He spent the rest of his life teaching and helping others. The religion of Buddhism is named after him.

Carving of the feet of the Buddha from Amaravati, India, 1st century B.C.

Foretelling the future

351

The Aztecs used obsidian (black volcanic glass) mirrors to help them foresee the future. For example, if a son or daughter was sick, parents would look at the child's reflection in the mirror. If it was clear, the child would get better, but if it was shadowy, the soul was lost and the child would die.

Aztec obsidian mirror from Mexico, 1325–1521 A.D.

352

The ancient Greeks believed in fate: your future was already mapped out for you and you couldn't change it. They visited places called oracles, where their futures could be foretold. The oracle at Delphi was the most famous. Here, after the sacrifice of a goat, the main priestess (the Pythia) would tell people their fates. According to some accounts she first inhaled some vapors rising from the ground, which made her speak in a strange voice.

353

The *I Jing* (Book of Changes) is the most ancient of Chinese texts. It gives advice for life based on cosmology and philosophy, and provides a system for explaining chance events. In ancient China the 64 hexagons of the *I Jing* were used to tell people's fortunes. Sticks, such as yarrow stalks, were thrown. The pattern they made when they fell was matched to a hexagram diagram, and the symbol was then interpreted.

Magic and curses

354

On the back of this beautiful silver Anglo-Saxon brooch is inscribed: "Ædwen owns me, may the Lord own her. May the Lord curse him who takes me from her, unless she gives me of her own free will."

Anglo–Saxon brooch.

355

Amulets are small objects that are worn or carried for good luck and protection against harm. Most cultures have used them, including the Egyptians, Romans, and Anglo–Saxons. The ancient Egyptians sometimes strung several onto jewelry, like this ancient version of a modern charm bracelet.

356

Found scratched on a piece of lead from Roman Britain: "I curse Tretia Maria and her life and mind and memory and liver and lungs mixed up together, and her words, thoughts, and memory."

Egyptian amulet bracelet.

357

This wax figure was used to cast a spell on the person it shows. It has a scroll in its back with the spell on it, and human hair pushed into its navel. Spells were used in ancient Egypt by priests and doctors, as well as ordinary people. The Egyptians were particularly worried that something might happen to them while they were asleep. Children would be given written spells to protect them from harm, such as being buried by a falling house or getting worms.

Sport

358

Gladiators were men (and occasionally women) who fought, sometimes to the death. In Roman arenas, they fought wild beasts and each other, purely for the pleasure of the onlookers.

Bronze figurine of a gladiator, 1st–2nd century A.D.

EIGHT FACTS
ABOUT GLADIATORS

359 For over 650 years, gladiatorial fights were held across the Roman Empire. Thousands were killed in this way during this time.

360 Under the empire, people came to expect magnificent spectacles. One show given by the Emperor Trajan lasted for 117 days, with nearly 5,000 pairs of gladiators.

361 Gladiators were usually slaves, and had no choice whether they fought or not.

362 At the end of a fight, the emperor would decide whether the gladiator's life should be spared by turning his thumb up or down for all to see.

363 At the first fight ever held in the Colosseum in Rome, 5,000 animals were killed.

364 The Colosseum was such a big arena that 60,000 people could fit into it to watch gladiator fights.

365 The Emperor Septimius Severus banned female gladiators in 200 A.D.

366 Eventually the cost in lives and money, together with objections from the Christian church, led to the contests being abolished in about 400 A.D.

367 TEN TYPES OF ROMAN GLADIATORS AND THEIR GEAR:

Retiarius (net and trident)
Secutor (short sword and long shield)
Murmillo (heavy armor and crested helmet)
Hoplomachus (spear and small round shield)
Thraex (curved sword and square shield)
Provocator (helmet with visor, sword, and large shield)
Eques (on horseback)
Essedarius (chariots)
Crupellarius (so heavily armed that if he fell over he couldn't get up again)
Venator (fought wild animals)

Murmillo's helmet, said to be from Pompeii, Italy. 1st century A.D.

368 TEN "STAGE NAMES" OF ROMAN GLADIATORS

Amethystus (amethyst)
Margarites (pearl)
Beryllus (beryl)
Smaragdus (emerald)
Leo (lion)
Ferox (ferocious)
Triumphus (the winner)
Tigris (tiger)
Invictus (unbeaten)
Rapidus (swift)

Secutor.

Murmillo.

369

The Vikings made ice-skates from the leg-bones of cows and horses. (They didn't skate just for fun—it made travel easier in winter, when the lakes and rivers froze.)

371

Lacrosse was first played by the Iroquois, a Native American tribe. It was introduced from Canada into Europe in the middle of the 19th century A.D.

370

The Romans loved watching chariot races. Every major city had a stadium where the races were held. The largest stadium by far was the Circus Maximus in Rome, which could hold 250,000 people. The winners of important races could become very wealthy celebrities, and the very passionate supporters of the various racing teams often ended up fighting each other. In Rome, the racing teams were the reds, whites, greens, and blues.

Model of a Roman two-horse racing chariot (*biga*), 1st–2nd century A.D.

Pair of Creek ballsticks from Oklahoma, around 1977.

372

Stickball is an American game played by the Creek tribe, who lived in Alabama and Georgia in the 18th and 19th centuries A.D. Each player held two long wooden sticks with leather nets at the end. A deerskin ball stuffed with hair was thrown and caught in the net. Two towns would play each other—the goals were 437 yards (400 m) apart, and each side had 62 players.

373

The word "gymnasium" comes from the Greek word gymnos, which means "naked," because Greek athletes competed naked.

374

The ancient Mayan and Aztec ballgame was a religious event, not just a sport. It was fast-paced and exciting, played on a special enclosed court. Two teams tried to keep the ball in the air, but were only allowed to use their elbows, hips, or knees to hit it. Players wore special protective clothing. You didn't want to be on the losing team, as occasionally they could be sacrificed.

The Aztec ballgame.

EIGHT EVENTS
of the ancient Olympic games

375

1 Chariot races
2 Horse races
3 Pentathlon (discus, javelin, jumping, running, wrestling)
4 Running
5 Wrestling
6 Boxing
7 *Pankration* (see fact 383 in the top 10 facts about the Olympic Games, opposite)
8 *Hoplitodromia* (see fact 381)

The *hoplitodromia*.

Amphora with runners.

Discus thrower.

Horse race.

Wrestlers.

Boxers.

Pankration.

TOP TEN FACTS
ABOUT THE OLYMPIC GAMES

376 Before the games began, the athletes, trainers, and their fathers had to swear to Zeus that they had trained for 10 months and that they would obey the rules.

377 If two neighboring Greek states were at war, they called a temporary truce during the Olympic Games so that their athletes could travel safely.

378 Chariot racing could be very dangerous. Forty chariots once entered an Olympic race and only one finished it, while the rest crashed.

379 Olympic wrestlers would wear tight-fitting caps so that their hair could not be grasped by their opponents.

380 The marathon as a sport (a race of 26 miles [38.5 km]) was not run in ancient Greece. It was actually invented in 1876 to commemorate the journey of the messenger in 490 B.C. who ran all the way to Athens from Marathon to tell of the Greek victory there.

381 The *hoplitodromia* was a race in which men had to run in full armor under the hot sun.

382 There was also the mule-cart race, which was only included for 14 Olympic games because of an ancient curse on mules bred within the sacred area of Olympia.

383 The *pankration* was a cross between boxing and wrestling. Any attack was allowed, except for biting or gouging out your opponent's eyes.

384 The greatest victory for an athlete was to win the Olympic crown, the prize for each event winner. The crown was a wreath of wild olive leaves cut from the tree, held as sacred to Zeus.

385 Number of women allowed to attend Olympic games: one, the priestess of Demeter. One writer said that any other women discovered at the games would be thrown off a cliff! Women had their own event at Olympia called the Heraia, which included only running races.

Model of ancient Olympia.

Towns and architecture

Towns

Ostrich egg cup from the ancient city of Ur, 2600–2200 B.C.

386

The very first cities included Ur, Eridu, and Nippur. They were built by the ancient Sumerians, who lived in Mesopotamia (now Iraq) over 4,000 years ago. No one knew that the ancient Sumerians even existed until about 100 years ago!

387

Babylon in Mesopotamia became an important city during the reign of Nebuchadnezzar II in the 6th century B.C. It had two groups of huge walls, and massive palaces and temples, including a towering central ziggurat (a kind of pyramid). It is said that at this time Nebuchadnezzar built the famous "hanging gardens of Babylon" (see page 126).

388

Roman towns seemed very sophisticated to the people they conquered. They were specially planned by architects to be like Rome, and included:

basilicas (large meeting halls)
bathhouses
town halls
theaters
amphitheaters

389

The center of any Roman town was the forum, a large open area used for markets, sport, and meetings. Around the forum were the main government buildings and the temple.

The temple of Saturn in the forum at Rome (painting by Francis Towne).

390

Roman towns included large public toilets. These had several spaces for men, women, and children to sit down together in the same room! Sometimes marble toilet seats were set over channels where flowing water made the first "flush" toilets. A shallow water channel in front of the seats held sponges attached to sticks for patrons to wipe themselves.

391

Most of the very poor in the city of Rome lived in dangerously rundown apartment blocks called *insulae*. These could be four or five floors high.

392

The government gave out free food handouts in Rome to the very poor. By the year 2 B.C., 200,000 people were registered for these handouts (see page 46, Food and drink).

393

During the reign of the Emperor Nero, a huge fire raged through the crowded wooden apartment blocks of Rome. Many of Nero's subjects were made homeless by the fire. Nero did not help them, but built himself a sumptuous palace called the Golden House shortly afterward. This did nothing for his popularity, and the tale spread that Nero had started the fire, then sung poetry while watching the flames.

395

On ancient Chinese streets, pedestrians had to give way to people carrying loads, who had to give way to empty sedan chairs, who had to give way to people in sedan chairs, who had to give way to horses. Everyone had to give way to important officials or wedding parties. Because it was polite to get down from your sedan chair or horse to greet a friend, sometimes pedestrians would hide their faces with fans to save their friends the trouble.

394

When the people of the town of Pompeii looked up into the sky on the morning of August 24, 79 A.D., they saw "a cloud rising in shape rather like a pine tree" over the volcano Vesuvius. This was the start of the eruption that was to kill hundreds of people, burying the town under 13 feet (4 m) of rubble and ash.

Wall painting from a house in Pompeii showing Odysseus and the Sirens.

396 SIX PIECES OF
ROMAN GRAFFITI FROM POMPEII

1 Jarinus, you live here! (*in the bathhouse*)
2 *Suspirium puellarum Celadus thraex:* Celadus the Thraex
   makes the girls sigh! (*in the barracks of the gladiators*)
3 Profit is happiness!
4 I've caught a cold!
5 Epaphra, you are bald!
6 O walls, you have held up so much tedious graffiti that I am
   amazed that you have not already collapsed in ruin!

397

From about 2600 to 1700 B.C. many towns
and cities were built on and around the
banks of the river Indus in northwest India.
These settlements covered a huge region,
twice as large as ancient Egypt. The cities of
the Indus Valley were solidly built out of
brick and stone. They had streets planned
on a grid system. Houses were two-storied,
each with its own bathing area that had
a drain emptying into the city's main
drainage system.

**Seal from the city of Harappa in
the Indus Valley, 2600–1900 B.C.**

398 SIX ANGLO–SAXON
place name endings and what they mean

1 **-burh** (modern *-burgh*) fort, later also fortified town
2 **-dun/down/den** down (hill)
3 **-ham** settlement
4 **-wic** farmstead (produce of a farm)
5 **-ton** farm or village
6 **-ford** river crossing

so:

Deptford deep ford
Oxford shallow ford where oxen crossed
Greenwich farm with fields
Woolwich farm with sheep

399 EIGHT VIKING
place name endings and what they mean

1 **-by** farm/village
2 **-thorpe** farm/village
3 **-toft** homestead
4 **-holme** island/reclaimed land
5 **-ness** headland
6 **-fell** mountain (fjell)
7 **-dale** valley (dal)
8 **-wick** bay (vik)

so:

Grimsby Grim's village
Lowestoft Loth or Lowe's homestead
Furness Fur's headland

400

When Viking and Saxon names became mixed up …

It was bound to happen as the Vikings and the Saxons started to marry each other and settle the land together. Grimston means "Grim's farm." Grim is a Viking name, but "ton" is the Saxon word for "farm." Because of this name, mixed Viking and Saxon place names are sometimes called Grimston hybrids (a hybrid is a mixture of two things).

401

The main Viking center in Britain for about 200 years was Jorvik (modern York). Archeologists have found many things left behind by the people who lived there, including jewelry, cups, bowls, coins, and even a wool sock. Viking Jorvik must have been a very smelly place—garbage was thrown into open drains in the street.

402

Aztec town life centered on the marketplace, where goods and gossip were exchanged. Aztec marketplaces were huge and bustling. Many different goods were bought and sold, from basic foods like maize to rare imports such as jaguar skins and precious stones.

403

The Aztec capital Tenochtitlan was built on an island in the middle of Lake Texcoco with four causeways (walkways) leading across the water to it. According to legend, their god Huitzilopochtli told them to build it where they saw an eagle land on a cactus. In the center of Tenochtitlan was a large square with a large pyramid, on which stood the temples of the gods Tlaloc and Huitzilopochtli.

A thousand years old and it still has all its teeth! A Viking comb from Jorvik, 9th–10th century A.D.

404

Ordinary people were not allowed into the Forbidden City in China. It was built in 1420 A.D. to be the center of government and to house the family of the emperor of China, right in the center of Beijing. The city of Beijing was built in a grid pattern (like modern American cities), so that people could get around easily. The streets ran from north to south and east to west in order to create good *feng shui*, bringing good luck and energy to the town.

405

Ancient Greece consisted of many different city–states. The two best known were probably Athens and Sparta; they were very different. During the Classical Period, the citizens of Athens had a say in the running of the city. Sparta, however, focused on producing good soldiers, and all Spartan male citizens were part of the army.

Architecture

406

Some Anglo–Saxons lived among the ruins of Roman towns. They decided that giants (whom they called Ents) must have built the huge crumbling remains.

407

The first cities of ancient Mesopotamia were built around huge temples called "ziggurats." These were made of brick and had steeply stepped sides.

408

The Maya of Mexico (300–900 A.D.) also built large cities and temples with stepped sides, steeper even than the ziggurats of Mesopotamia. Mayan legend told that the towering Temple of the Magician at Uxmal was built in one night single-handedly by a magician–god named Itzamna.

409

Greek temples are famous for their impressive columns. The portico (the porch with the columns at the front) of the British Museum copies a Greek style of architecture. The tall pillars gradually taper at the top so that they look straight and even when you look up at them.

The front of the British Museum, which is based on the temple of Athena at Priene.

The remains of the ziggurat of Ur.

THE SEVEN WONDERS
of the ancient world

410

The Pyramids of Giza, Egypt,
around 2551–2472 B.C.

The Great Pyramid was built by King
Khufu. It was almost 500 ft (150 m) high,
and used over 2,000,000 stone blocks. The
capstone at the top was coated with gold.
To this day, no one knows exactly how the
Egyptians managed to lift the huge blocks
into place.

411

The Hanging Gardens of Babylon
(modern Iraq), 605–562 B.C.

The most mysterious of the wonders,
because we don't know what they looked
like. However, they were probably built on
a series of steps, giving a hanging effect as
foliage trailed over the edge of each level.

412

The Temple of Artemis at Ephesus,
Turkey, around 550–325 B.C.

Famous because of its huge size—
377 ft x 170 ft (115 m x 55 m)—and its
many decorated pillars, but also because
it contained a vast statue of the goddess
Artemis made from gold, silver, ebony,
and black stone.

413

The Statue of Zeus at Olympia, Greece, around 430 B.C.

This masterpiece stood in the temple of Zeus at Olympia. It was around 39 ft (12 m) high, plated with gold and ivory. It showed the god sitting on a decorated throne with his hands outstretched.

414

The Colossus of Rhodes, Greece, 294–282 B.C.

This was a huge—105 ft (32 m) high—bronze statue of the sun god Helios, built by the harbor in the city of Rhodes to commemorate the end of a long siege.

415

The Mausoleum of Halicarnassus (modern Bodrum), Turkey, around 353 B.C.

Built as a tomb for King Mausollos by his widow Artemisia, our word for a large tomb—mausoleum— is taken from his name. It included 36 marble columns and a stepped roof, topped with a huge marble chariot pulled by four horses.

Statue from the Mausoleum, probably Mausollos.

416

The Pharos (Lighthouse) of Alexandria, Egypt, 297–283 B.C.

The lighthouse stood on the island of Pharos in the harbor at Alexandria. At 351 ft (110 m) high, only the Great Pyramid of Giza was taller in the ancient world.

Fragment of a column from the Temple of Artemis.

127

Houses

417

The poorest Romans lived in one- or two-room apartments. Essential services such as fires for cooking and water for washing were provided outside, and were used by a number of families.

418

Many rich Romans had villas, country houses where they lived for all or part of the year. Some villas had fine gardens with pools and fountains; others were working farms with bakeries and oil presses.

419

Roman houses had central heating. This came from a *hypocaust*. Slaves stoked a fire in the cellar, and the hot air from the fire would flow up through spaces underneath the floor of the house. Central heating from hypocausts was especially used in the most northern provinces of the empire, like Germany and Britain, which the Romans could find very chilly.

420

Greek houses were built around courtyards. Many family activities, such as food preparation and cooking, took place in the courtyard, especially in summer. Inside the house, the floors were earth beaten flat. There was very little furniture and the windows were small. There was no heating except for the central fire, used for cooking; oil lamps provided only a little light.

421

Aztec houses were made of earth and straw bricks called *adobe*, and built around courtyards. The Aztecs used chairs and sleeping mats made from reeds.

422

The floors and walls of houses owned by wealthy Romans were decorated with paintings and mosaics—pictures made from tiny pieces of tile called *tesserae*. These often had a central picture surrounded by patterns. The Leadenhall Street mosaic shows Bacchus riding on a tiger.

Leadenhall Street Mosaic from London, Britain, 1st or 2nd century A.D.

Painting of a garden pool, from the tomb–chapel of a man called Nebamun, around 1350 B.C.

424

Shady gardens made a welcome retreat from the hot sun in ancient Egypt, but only the richest Egyptians could afford them. Here they grew vegetables, flowers, and grapes, and ponds were filled with fish and waterlilies. Temples had the biggest gardens, so that they could grow all the flowers and plants needed as offerings to the gods.

423

Houses in ancient Egypt were built of mud brick, which was plastered and whitewashed to reflect the sun, and had tiny windows to keep them cool. The houses did not have much furniture, but there were benches to eat and sleep on. When it was very hot, people sometimes slept on the flat roof.

Model of a house from Egypt, about 1900 B.C.

War
The Roman army

425

A century: a Roman centurion was in charge of 80 men (not 100, despite the name).

426

A legion: the number of soldiers in a Roman legion was 5,000. The legions were the backbone of the Roman army. They were heavily armed and strictly disciplined. A young man would sign up at about age 18 for about 25 years' service. In return, he got good pay, and he would be granted Roman citizenship and given money or land when he retired.

Bronze statue of a Roman legionary, 2nd century A.D.

427

Auxiliaries: auxiliaries were non-Roman citizens recruited from conquered countries. Auxiliaries often had military skills that the legionary soldiers didn't. They might be expert archers, slingshot men, or cavalry. They did not get paid as much as legionaries, but when they retired they were granted Roman citizenship.

428

Equipment: Even on a 20-mile (30-km) training march a Roman legionary would carry a huge amount of equipment. This included:

SWORD   TURF-CUTTER
DAGGER   PAN
SHIELD   DISH
KNIFE   CHAIN
SAW   CLOAK
BASKET   FOOD AND DRINK
AXE   (FOR THREE DAYS)

Iron sword, made in the 1st century A.D.

Roman cavalrymen.

429

Roman soldiers on the march drank vinegar. This wasn't as terrible as it sounds. It was actually cheap wine blended with water into a refreshing drink called *posca*.

430

The Emperor Claudius used elephants in the invasion of Britain. They must have terrified the native Britons, and were used successfully in the conquest of Camulodunum (modern Colchester).

431

In the city–state of Sparta, fighting was taken extremely seriously. Having joined the army at the age of seven, all boys and young men lived in barracks until they were 30 years old. Even if they got married, they could only visit their wives in secret.

433

"Viking" means "pirate." The Vikings earned this name by raiding and fighting abroad. At home the Vikings were farmers, but they discovered that piracy could be a more profitable career. They started with closer neighbors in Britain and Europe, but then journeyed to Iceland, Greenland, and even as far as North America. To the south, they reached Jerusalem and Baghdad.

432

The foot soldiers called *hoplites* were the most important part of a Greek army during the later part of ancient Greek history. *Hoplites* carried a bronze shield and iron weapons, and were protected by armor. Some threw short spears at the enemy, and some fought with long thrusting spears.

Greek soldiers fighting with spears and shields.

***Hoplite's* helmet from Greece, 460 B.C.**

Viking spearhead, 9th–10th century A.D.

434

The first Viking raid on Britain was in 793 A.D., when they attacked the rich monastery of Lindisfarne, unprotected on its island in northeast England. A priest wrote: "Never before has such a terror come to Britain as this … nor was it thought possible that such an invasion could come from the sea."

436

Samurai armor. This suit of armor was made between the 16th and 19th centuries A.D., and includes a metal breastplate, to stop bullets!

435

In Aztec Mexico, one of the most prestigious jobs a man could have was that of a warrior, and the two top groups of noble warriors were called the jaguars and the eagles. To join one of these, a warrior had to take more than four prisoners in battle.

An Aztec eagle–warrior, 1325–1521 A.D.

The first samurai warriors in Japan fought for the emperor in the eighth century A.D. Gradually they gained power for themselves, and in 1192 A.D. the first samurai emperor took control. The samurai were highly trained fighters, usually Zen Buddhists, who lived very simply and with great self-control. They were always ready to die for their cause.

Weapons and armor

437

Celtic men from western Europe from around 700 B.C. would rush into battle shouting. They made themselves look more frightening by combing lime into their hair so that it stuck up in spikes. They also painted patterns on their skins with a blue dye made from the woad plant. It must have been a terrifying sight to have them charging.

438

Greek fire was a substance that would burn fiercely in air and on water. It would even burn under water! It could not be extinguished. Greek fire was first used by the Byzantines in a sea battle in 673 A.D. What it was made from was a secret, and no one now knows exactly what was in Greek fire. Possibly one ingredient was naptha, a crude form of petrol.

Sword from the ship burial at Sutton Hoo, early 7th century A.D.

439

As a Spartan man went off to war his wife would give him his shield, saying that he should return "with this or upon it." If he came back with his shield, he was alive and safe. If he came back on his shield, he was dead, and was being carried home in honor by other soldiers. If he came back without his shield, it would be assumed that he had run away from battle, and he would be banished or even executed.

440

The weapon most commonly used by Anglo–Saxon warriors was the spear.

441

Few Anglo–Saxon warriors could afford swords. Swords could be given names. They were often passed down from father to son, or buried with their owner when he died.

442

The first Europeans to reach West Africa were the Portuguese, who arrived in the kingdom of Benin (now Nigeria) between 1482 and 1496 A.D. They introduced guns to the Africans, and became rich trading with them.

Model of a Portuguese soldier holding a gun from Benin, 17th century A.D.

443

Japanese swordmakers were very skilled. Fine blades were made by folding and hammering, then heating the metal and plunging it into cold water. This meant that the blade was strong but sharp enough to cut through armor. A samurai warrior's sword was so important to him that there are many different words in Japanese just for the different parts of a sword: the pattern on the edge of the blade, the fine point, the curve toward the hilt, and so on.

444

Gunpowder was invented in China in the second or third century, probably as a by-product of an alchemist's experiments. The Chinese first used gunpowder in warfare in 904 A.D. By 1132 A.D. it was used to fire projectiles, such as arrows, from bamboo tubes. The explosive power of the gunpowder when it was lit hurled the missiles very effectively at the enemy.

Sieges

445

In 71 A.D. the Romans besieged the city of Jerusalem. The siege ended when the Romans set fire to the Jewish Temple. They probably killed tens of thousands of people. Most of the dead were Jews who had gathered to celebrate Passover.

Scene from the Nereid monument showing soldiers scaling a city wall, 390–380 B.C.

446

Genghis Khan and other Mongol rulers were very successful at besieging cities. One tactic was to use catapults to launch the corpses of plague victims over the walls. These would quickly spread disease—an early form of biological warfare.

448

Ladders with wheels are the first known siege weapons. They are shown on ancient Egyptian tomb carvings from as early as 2400 B.C. The Egyptians used them to attack Canaanite towns.

447

The story of the Trojan War tells how, after a 10-year siege, the city of Troy was finally captured by the Greeks. They hid their best warriors inside a huge wooden horse, then pretended to sail away, leaving it outside the city gates. The Trojans believed that it would bring them luck if they offered the horse to the goddess Athena, and dismantled a wall section to get it into the city. While they feasted, the warriors inside the horse sprang out, and the Greeks took the Trojans by surprise.

A model wooden horse greets visitors at Troy today.

449

Alexander the Great conducted many successful sieges. The Phoenician city of Tyre was heavily fortified and built on an island .6 miles (1 km) off the coast. It was considered impossible to defeat. Alexander built a wide causeway out to the island, then attacked the walls with catapults and stone throwers. Tyre still managed to hold out for seven months before surrendering in 332 B.C.

450

The ancient Assyrians were skilled in war, and wall carvings from their palaces show sieges in progress. Their battering rams were sophisticated, and they even had something like early tanks! They were wooden engines on wheels, and from the tops archers could shoot over city walls.

Punishing prisoners (probably flaying them alive) from the siege of Lachish, 701 B.C.

SEVEN ANCIENT
SIEGE WEAPONS

451 Battering ram: used to break down gates and walls. Could have a protective roof and contain archers or other soldiers.

452 Catapult: could fire anything, from stones and bundles of wood that had been set on fire to infected corpses. The Roman *onagar* catapult was named after a wild ass because of its kicking power.

453 Flamethrower: these threw out a long stream of fire. The flames could have come from a mysterious concoction called "Greek fire."

454 Siege tower: a tall tower, usually with wheels, which attackers would push up to the walls of the besieged city.

455 Trebuchet: much more accurate than catapults, these could fire missiles over long distances or batter down walls.

456 Agger: Roman earthen ramp, built to scale walls.

457 Ballista: powerful crossbow first developed in ancient Greece.

458

Demetrius I of Macedon invented an incredible siege machine called the *helepolis* ("taker of cities"), which was plated with iron and stood nine stories (131 ft or 40 m) high. He used this to conquer Rhodes in 305–304 B.C.

Some famous military campaigns

459

Hannibal was one of the few commanders to oppose the power of Rome successfully. He gathered together an army—including elephants—and marched from Spain through southern France and over the mountains into northern Italy. Here he won many battles. However, he never had enough power to attack Rome itself, and his campaign was eventually defeated. He was very skilled at tactics, and the Romans even adopted some of his ideas themselves. Hannibal was a general of the city of Carthage, a city on the coast of North Africa (now Tunisia).

A coin from Carthage showing Hannibal on an elephant, 230 B.C.

460

Each Greek city–state had its own army, and these often fought against each other. The Peloponnesian War between Athens and Sparta lasted 27 years, from 431 B.C. until 404 B.C. The Spartans won by laying siege to Athens, then breaking in when the city was weakened by the plague.

461

The Aztec Conquest

Hernándo Cortès of Spain landed on the eastern shore of Mexico in 1519 A.D. with around 600 men, 17 horses, and 10 cannon. Realizing that he was greatly outnumbered, he burned most of his fleet of ships so that his soldiers could not desert. He made allies of the Tlaxcalans, who were enemies of the Aztecs, and marched upon Tenochtitlan,

463
The Norman Conquest

When Edward the Confessor died, Harold Godwinson was crowned king of England. William, Duke of Normandy, was enraged because he believed Edward had wanted him to be the next king. William also said Harold had made a solemn promise to support him. William led an army across the Channel and faced Harold at the battle of Hastings, October 14, 1066 A.D. The fight was close, but Harold was eventually killed when an arrow shot by one of William's archers hit him in the eye.

464

William of Normandy wasn't the only ruler interested in becoming king of England. Just before the battle of Hastings, Harold had had to march north to Yorkshire very quickly to fight his brother Tostig and Harald Hardrada, king of Norway. The battle of Stamford Bridge (September 1066 A.D.) was a victory for Harold, but instead of being able to rest his men, he had to march them back at top speed down the length of England to fight William!

Turquoise mosaic mask of Quetzalcoatl.

462

the Aztec capital. The emperor Motecuhzoma (Moctezuma) II and his people thought that he was the god Quetzalcoatl and so did not attack him until it was too late. Instead they gave him gifts, including a mask of Quetzalcoatl. Thousands of Aztecs including Motecuhzoma were killed.

An Aztec poem about the conquest:

Broken spears lie in the roads
we have torn our hair in our grief
the houses are roofless now, and
their walls are red with blood.

There were probably about 20 million people living in ancient Mexico in 1500 A.D., including the Aztecs, Maya, and Mixtecs. One hundred years later, there were only about one or two million native people left. Europeans had brought new diseases, war, and slavery, with dreadful results.

Writing

Clay tablet with pictograms recording the allocation of beer, around 3100–3000 B.C.

465

The oldest written language in the world is probably ancient Sumerian. The oldest inscription dates back to about 3600 B.C. The first written signs were pictograms (picture signs). These were gradually simplified and developed into cuneiform script.

466

Ancient Sumerians used a reed stylus to make wedge-shaped signs. ("Cuneiform" means "wedge-shaped.") The clay dried into hard tablets, which have survived very well over the centuries. At first Sumerian people kept day-to-day records and wrote down laws. Later they also recorded prayers, stories, and legends.

A boy's schoolwork is written on this clay tablet in cuneiform script. From around 1900–1700 B.C.

467

The people living in the Indus Valley of India over 4,000 years ago developed a writing system based on pictographs—which we still cannot decipher.

Egyptian funeral stela inscription giving the name and titles of Horiraa, an important priest of Ptah at Memphis.

468

The ancient Egyptians developed their hieroglyphic picture-writing more than 5,000 years ago. "Hieroglyphs" means "sacred carvings" because the writing usually appeared in sacred places such as monuments and temples. A hieroglyph can stand for a sound, an idea, or a whole word. Some hieroglyphic signs are complicated, but some are quite simple. The hieroglyph for "town" is a circle with two roads crossing it.

The hieroglyph for "town."

469

Egyptian hieroglyphs can be read either from right to left or left to right. How do you know which way? Look at which direction the animals and birds are facing, and read toward them.

These beautifully colored hieroglyphs should be read from left to right. They are written on a coffin of the Middle Kingdom Period.

141

The Rosetta Stone, carved in 196 B.C.

471

Until the Rosetta Stone was discovered in 1799 A.D., nobody could read Egyptian hieroglyphs. The Rosetta Stone had the same text on it in three different scripts: hieroglyphs, demotic (everyday Egyptian), and ancient Greek. Scholars used their knowledge of Greek to crack the code.

472

There was an international race to decipher the Rosetta Stone code! Two scholars, Thomas Young, an English physicist, and the Frenchman Jean-François Champollion, both competed to decipher the Rosetta Stone first. Young deduced that some of the letters made up the sounds of the name of Ptolemy V, but it was Champollion who then realized that the other hieroglyphs made up the sounds of letters and syllables.

470

It's probably the best technological invention ever! The alphabet was most likely invented in ancient Palestine and Syria around 3,600 years ago. As the idea was passed across the world from person to person, different alphabets developed, such as the Greek alphabet, the Cyrillic alphabet, and the Roman alphabet, which is used to write many western languages today.

ABCDEFGHIJKLMNOPQRSTUVWXYZ

473

The Greek alphabet is the ancestor of all modern European alphabets. It was developed around 900 B.C. from the Phoenician alphabet. It was the first to use vowel sounds as well as consonants, which made it extremely flexible and useful. Classical Greek had 24 letters, the first being alpha, and the last omega.

The ancient Greek alphabet.

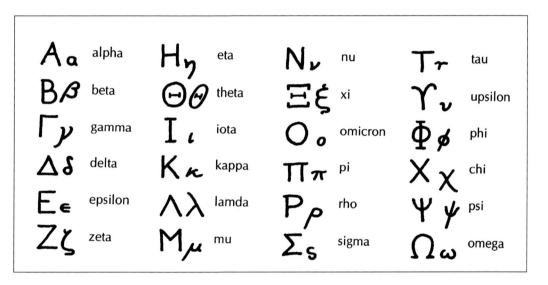

A α alpha	H η eta	N ν nu	T τ tau
B β beta	Θ θ theta	Ξ ξ xi	Υ υ upsilon
Γ γ gamma	I ι iota	O ο omicron	Φ φ phi
Δ δ delta	K κ kappa	Π π pi	X χ chi
E ε epsilon	Λ λ lamda	P ρ rho	Ψ ψ psi
Z ζ zeta	M μ mu	Σ ς sigma	Ω ω omega

474

Early Greek writing was sometimes known as *boustrophedon*, or "ox-turning," because it was written left to right then right to left, like an ox going backward and forward plowing.

475

Romans wrote and spoke Latin, which is one of the roots of today's English language (and many other European languages).

476

Over 3,000 years ago in ancient Crete, they used three different writing systems. One of them—called Linear B—was cracked in 1952 by architect Michael Ventris. He proved that it was based on ancient Greek, a discovery that caused great surprise at the time. Two of the Cretan writing systems, Linear A and a kind of hieroglyphs only found in Crete, are still a mystery!

Part of a tablet showing Linear B writing from Crete. It was written around 1450–1400 B.C.

477

The Aztecs wrote everything down, which is where we get our detailed knowledge of their civilization from. They used a form of picture-writing that recorded numbers, dates, and names—but they had no way of representing sounds or parts of words, so their writing cannot really be called a whole script in the same way as Egyptian hieroglyphs.

478

Most Anglo–Saxons could not read and write. When they did, however, they used *runes*, a kind of picture writing. Their alphabet was called the *futhorc*. The Viking used a similar kind of alphabet. Runes are designed for carving on wood, stone, or metal, rather than writing down. Sometime the runes were thought to have magic powers.

479

Some Aztec pictograms are for things, such as "mountain" or "house," and some are for ideas, such as a temple with its roof off for "defeat."

MOUNTAIN

HOUSE

DEFEAT

Anglo–Saxon runes.

| f | u | th | o | r | k | g | w | h | j | i | n | i | p |

| x | s | t | b | e | ng | m | l | d | oe | a | ae | y | ea |

480

Modern Chinese people can read ancient documents fairly easily, because Chinese has changed very little since it started being written down in about 1300 B.C. Chinese uses over 50,000 pictograms in all. Luckily you only need to know three thousand to read a newspaper, but as you can imagine, Chinese children spend a lot of time practicing their writing. In the past, Chinese characters were read from the top down and right to left.

482

Muslims everywhere learn to read the Qu'ran in Arabic script, as this was the language used by Muhammad's followers to write it down originally. The beautiful flowing lines of Arabic script are used to decorate the walls of mosques, as well as many different objects.

481

The art of calligraphy ("beautiful writing") was held in high esteem in China because of its political importance. The basic tools used by the calligrapher were paper, writing brush, ink, and an inkstone, on which the dry ink would be mixed with water. These were known as "the four treasures of the scholar's studio."

483

An Arab historian wrote that Muslim scribes had to look after their equipment: "It is necessary for the scribe to do his utmost to adorn the pen–box, to make it excellent and to look after it." The owner of this pen–box has decorated it with a verse from the Qu'ran.

Pen–box from Iraq, 1230–50 A.D.

484

The ancient Maya were able to record more detail than the Aztecs. Mayan writing is complicated and was only deciphered in the last century; we still cannot understand all of it. They used over 800 glyphs (picture-signs), which stand for sounds, words, or whole ideas.

Maya glyphs on a doorway listing nine generations of rulers, 600–800 A.D.

Writing equipment

485

Instead of using books, the ancient Chinese recorded things in scrolls—long lengths of paper that unrolled.

Part of the Admonitions Scroll from China, 6th–8th century A.D.

486

Because the ancient Chinese wrote on paper, some of their old documents have disintegrated and are lost, though others survive on bamboo or carved in stone.

487

Scribes in ancient Egypt wrote on papyrus, a kind of paper made from reeds. They used a brush made from rushes, and chewed the end to separate the fibers. The brush was dipped into water, then wiped across a tablet of ink. Writing was mainly in black, with red sometimes used for highlighting.

488

The first libraries were put together in ancient Sumer around 2700 B.C. They contained clay tablets covered in cuneiform writing.

489

The hieroglyphic sign for "write" was made up from pictures of a scribe's palette and brush case.

490

Early Greek books were long rolls of papyrus with the title at the end inside so it was less likely to be damaged.

493

Ogham is the oldest known Celtic writing system. The Ogham alphabet was used in Ireland from about the fourth century, and sometimes in Cornwall, Scotland, and Wales, where Irish people settled. Straight lines and notches were carved down the sharp edges of stone or wood. There were twenty letters in Ogham. Only very short inscriptions have been found using Ogham.

491

Aztec and Mayan books are called *codices*. They are made from long strips of fig bark folded like a concertina, with covers made of jaguar skin. Very few original books survive.

Codex Zouche–Nuttall, Mixtec, 1200–1521 A.D.

492

There were hundreds of thousands of Aztec and Mayan books, made from animal skin or tree–bark paper, but most were destroyed by the Spaniards after they conquered Mexico. The Spaniards thought that books about the Aztec religion were evil.

494

Paper was invented in China in the 1st century B.C.

495

Wax tablets were the most common way of writing in the Roman world. A layer of wax was spread over a flat surface, such as a small piece of wood. Marks could be made on the wax with a sharp stylus made of metal or bone. When the message was old, the surface could be smoothed to use again.

Wooden base for a Roman wax writing tablet and two styli (pens). 1st or 2nd century A.D.

496

To stop the wrong people from reading their letters, people in ancient times used a variety of seals. A popular type of seal to keep a letter shut used a blob of melted wax. When it was soft, this could be stamped with the owner's special mark.

Seal shaped like a lion's paw with animal head from Anatolia (modern Turkey), 1920–1800 B.C.

497

The first books in Britain were religious texts, handwritten in Latin and illustrated by monks, such as the scholars at Lindisfarne monastery in Northumberland, who wrote the Lindisfarne Gospels. There was no paper, so they wrote on specially treated animal skins. One very big book used the skins of fifty sheep.

498

Animal skins prepared for writing are usually called "parchment." Mostly they are skins of sheep, calves, or goats, though sometimes skins of animals such as antelopes or ostriches were used. Vellum is top-grade parchment, made from the skins of very young calves.

499

Mesopotamian clay tablets were sometimes put into clay "envelopes" before being sent. The envelopes were sealed with cylinder seals. These were small stone cylinders carved with patterns or pictures, which would be rolled along the clay tablet, leaving a mark behind. This letter is from one brother to another, telling of how winter has come and his family has no food, clothes, or fuel. It was put into an envelope before being sent.

Clay tablet and its "envelope" (below). Around 1850 B.C.

500

Archeologists have found Roman documents written in ink on wooden tablets. One wooden tablet was an invitation to a birthday party from one lady to another. It was found at Vindolanda Fort on Hadrian's Wall in northern Britain.

Birthday party invitation. Around 97–103 A.D.

Find out more

Of course, there are many more than 500 things to know about history. If you'd like to discover more, here are some suggestions to get you started.

Books

Mike Corbishley, *The British Museum Illustrated Encyclopaedia of Ancient Rome*, British Museum Press 2003

Geraldine Harris and Delia Pemberton, *The British Museum Illustrated Encyclopaedia of Ancient Egypt*, British Museum Press 2005

Carolyn Howitt, *The British Museum Quiz Book of the Ancient World*, British Museum Press 2004

Sean Sheehan, *The British Museum Illustrated Encyclopaedia of Ancient Greece*, British Museum Press 2002

Katharine Wiltshire, *The British Museum Timeline of the Ancient World*, British Museum Press 2004

Web Sites

Visit the British Museum web site **www.thebritishmuseum.ac.uk**, which has lots of information and activities for families and children in the Explore section.

You can also explore these fantastic interactive web sites:

www.ancientchina.co.uk
www.earlyimperialchina.co.uk
www.mughalindia.co.uk
www.ancientcivilizations.co.uk
www.ancientegypt.co.uk
www.ancientgreece.co.uk
www.mesopotamia.co.uk
www.ancientindia.co.uk